7:55 A.M.

7:55 A.M.

By Lee Charles Daniels

Published by
MIDNIGHT EXPRESS BOOKS

7:55 A.M.

Published by
MIDNIGHT EXPRESS BOOKS
POBox 69
Berryville AR 72616
(870) 210-3772
MEBooks1@yahoo.com

7:55 A.M.

By Lee Charles Daniels

FORWARD

About a year ago, I was invited by the University of Nebraska, (Prairie Schooner) to submit a short, romantic story for an upcoming contest; the story was to be fifteen to twenty pages long.

After giving this invitation much thought (about forty minutes), I picked up my quill and paper and sat down at my desk and waited as I dipped my new quill in its ink well for an inspiration to strike. The following is the story I did not write.

Once my quill made its first mark on the paper, the story very much wrote itself, with my hand holding and dipping the quill in the ink well one stroke after the next.

The characters quickly took on a life of their own instructing me how and what to write. To say that I wrote the story would be an untruth when it was Catlin and Randy who are the real authors of 7:55 A.M.. And to them, I am thankful for a story well thought and filled with the exciting twists and turns I expect out of all my characters.

IT WAS THE LAST WEEK OP APRIL, 1964 AND A FRIDAY ....

Catlin Hyde was sixteen and restless as she stood on the street corner. Her long dark brown hair fluttered freely as the breeze from the many passing cars caught it. Her eyes glistened with hope that Bobby would come by to pick her up.

Bobby Bargin was the love of her life. His nickname was 'BB', but she loved calling him by his Christian name.

Bobby and she shared special birthdays, his was on Valentine's Day, February 14, 1946, her's was on Easter Sunday, March 28, 1948.

The morning President Kennedy was killed, she laid in the arms of Bobby as they made love for the first time. A day she would never forget, and would relive each morning.

Catlin stood at the corner of Edgewood and Roosevelt Boulevard on Jacksonville's west side waiting for the school bus that would eventually take her to Robert E. Lee High School, that is if Bobby didn't show up first.

Standing next to Catlin was her best friend, Mary Adele, whose red curls only enhanced her beauty and her emerald green eyes. Both girls stood several inches over Mary's sister, Anna, who was a year younger than Mary, and another six months older than Catlin.

There were more than a dozen young people waiting for the bus which was now running late as the new Cinderella Watch Bobby had given her the night before said it was 7:55 A.M.

The first scream sounded surreal. Catlin didn't have time to turn but when she lifted her eyes it was long too late to react.

Chapter 1

Randy Carr was just eighteen years old. He had had his driver's license for just one year and had been driving without the states mandatory youthful driver's restrictions for only three weeks.

As a senior at Robert E. Lee High School, he was less than two months from graduation. The Senior Prom was just a couple of weeks away with finals that would begin the week after that. His parents had given him his graduation present early, a bright red Ford Mustang convertible, the one he had picked out two weeks before Christmas.

Randy was the oldest of five kids and was looked up to by four sisters. Since Randy had the third car in the family, his sisters expected him to ferry each of them to the mall or school or where ever they wanted to go, but as fate would have it, Randy had taken a job in a small law firm to help pay for the insurance that he was required to have on his pride and joy.

As things turned out, Randy had little time for girlfriends; hell, he barely had time to eat between working crazy hours doing research and school. He didn't have time to even look for a friend, let alone a girlfriend.

Having a car gave Randy the feeling every young person gets when they are starting out on their own for the first time.

This morning, Randy had taken Edgewood down to Roosevelt Blvd, turning left towards downtown and school. He caught the light at the railroad tracks just before turning left and his eye wondered to a pretty girl standing on the side of the road holding several school books.

Seeing her dark brown hair, he noticed her old fashioned dress, thinking to himself, "not bad". The time was now 7:55 A.M..

A whisper of wind
Blows gently by, softly
Playing her name.
He sees the beauty
That existed then
Now only a silhouette
Through a lighted gown.

The light changed and he made his turn and proceeded on to school, having just enough time to say hello to a few friends before the school bell rang.

That night he had to finish some research for an upcoming trial and he worked with other young staffers until nearly three in the morning.

By seven, he had only two hours of sleep. Betty Carr, his mother, knowing how hard he'd been working and studying decided to let him sleep another fifteen minutes and made him a high protein breakfast and had Tammy, his younger sister set a place for him at the kitchen table as she woke her son up.

Randy's eyes were a tad blood shot and he found his Visine in the bathroom medicine cabinet. Applying the saline to his tired eyes, he allowed the soothing feeling of it to envelope his entire being for five more minutes, then showered, got dressed and went downstairs to grab a hot cup of coffee and a glass of orange juice before hitting the back door.

Betty and Tammy were waiting for him as he entered the spacious kitchen. Before the bat wing doors could close behind him, the whiff of fried bacon had reached his nose. His mouth watered before his eyes ever saw the special breakfast they had laid out for him.

The first words out of his mouth was "I don't have . ."

That was as far as he got. Betty slipped a large chunk of bacon into his mouth and he was then handed a fresh glass of Tammy's personally squeezed orange and strawberry juice as she pulled the chair out from the kitchen table as Betty gently, but firmly guided her sleepy son into the non-cushioned chair. He had been hooked, and he knew it. *"Sometimes,"* he thought to himself that *"it is better to just sit back and enjoy the little pleasures that life has to offer"* then he did!

At 7:20 that morning Betty informed her son that he was going to have to take Tammy to school before heading to his own school two miles out of the way but after the great breakfast he readily agreed.

Tammy got in the car and then asked her brother "Can you put the top down?"

"Sure, anything for one of the best cooks east of the mighty Mississippi," he jokingly told her as he released the roof lock- down latches. It took all of about thirty seconds and they were off. The clock on the dash said it was 7:40am.

At 7:47, Randy pulled in front of Edgewood Middle School, with a beaming redheaded little sister calling to her friends to come meet her older grown-up brother. "Hey, Tam, I've gotta go or I'll be late for class," he begged her.

Relenting, she kissed him on the cheek and slipped out of the car. The time now was 7:50 A.M.

At exactly 7:55 A.M., he found himself sitting at the same red light at Edgewood and Roosevelt. His mind clicked and he looked to his right to find the same pretty girl standing in the same spot holding a bundle of school books. "What the heck!" he said to himself, then pulled over to the curb and addressed the girl, "Are you going to Lee High?"

"Yeah," she answered him politely.

"Wanna ride?" Randy asked.

"Okay," she said as she opened the car door and got in.

"My name is Randy Carr. I'm a senior. How about you?"

"I'm Catlin Hyde, a junior," she offered.

"You must live pretty close around here because I see you almost every morning," Randy told her, after a brief few minutes.

"2763 Darcy, a few blocks over," she told him.

"Have you been going to the General long?" Randy asked.

"Yeah, it seems like forever," she answered.

"I know what you mean, I was just wondering, I can't remember seeing you around school before," Randy told her.

Catlin's dress was pale blue, nothing special, but it was old fashioned enough to be quite pretty on her. The neckline wasn't cut too deep, but just deep enough for him to notice the fullness of her breast. She wore a gold cross that had small diamonds imbedded in it. Her face was clear and unblemished and her earrings matched the cross.

Then he noticed she hadn't put her seatbelt on. "Better buckle up," he told her. "Can't afford a ticket."

She looked at him kinda funny, like as though she didn't understand.

Reaching over her at the next light, he drew her seatbelt across her lap and clicked it into place.

She seemed startled, but not overly so, seeing how he too had one on, as she watched him first hit the release and watched it spring back as he reached across her before putting his back on. The light changed and they drove on.

Randy had taken in the thin one inch belt around her slim waist that he now noticed matched her dark blue shoes, and thought to himself, "*Do people still wear matching clothes? A rare novelty.*"

The socks she wore were white and folded down over her ankles. Her legs were smooth and clean. It had been a long time since Randy had had any kind of girlfriend; he liked the way Catlin's hair shined and blew in the open air, thinking she must spend a lot of time brushing it to get it to shine like that.

They were still more than a mile from Lee when Randy began telling her about how he wanted to study law, and because he was a senior, the school let him out at 1P.M. so that he could earn extra credits by working as a clerk for the Dunleavy and Smith Law firm on the Southside.

She seemed interested and listened as he spoke of how corporate lawyers make good money guiding clients through the course of doing business.

"Do you plan on specializing in any particular field after you graduate?" he asked.

"It's still early," she told him, "and I haven't made up my mind yet. I'll probably get married and start a family, but who knows; maybe I'll find something special to get into."

Her smile was infectious causing him to smile too.

"My mom's a Registered Nurse," she told him.

Catlin began telling Randy over the next ten minutes about her boyfriend, Bobby, and the plans they made. "Bobby is gonna be an architectural designer, or engineer. Last year he designed a super structure in miniature for an exhibition and won a scholarship to the University of South Florida."

While Randy listened intently, his heart dropped a notch or two. When they arrived at the General, he parked the car. Catlin seemed interested in how when Randy pushed a button, the top came up and all but locked itself into place at the top of the windshield.

"That's nifty," she said. "Thank you for the ride, maybe I'll see you later," she said as she disappeared into a small gaggle of students.

Randy looked deep into the crowd of students, but she vanished into thin air. During lunch, Randy looked all throughout the lunch room for Catlin but gave up and headed for his history class knowing he'd not

9

see her anymore that day, but couldn't get her out of his head.

That afternoon and evening, Randy worked hard while at the law office but his mind was on the pretty girl. He and his coworkers worked hard and long into the   night. At 3:45 the next morning, his boss, Larry Smith, brother of Attorney William Smith, the senior partner, walked in to find all the high school clerks hard at work without even knowing what time it was, then sent everyone home.

Randy knew better than to try going to bed, so when he got home, he took a shower and sat down at his computer and spent two hours going over his school assignments, but his mind was still on Catlin.

At 7 am, his mom was asking about the time he came in saying, "It isn't right to make kids work that late."

"Mom," Randy said, "today is Friday, and I've got the whole weekend off, so it's alright."

By 7:45, he had dressed and was out the door. The temperature was already near 75° so he put the top down. He also hit the local Micky D's at Edgewood and Thornix, which was three blocks from Roosevelt Boulevard.

He had hoped he'd hit the busstop in time to pick Catlin up for school. At Micky D's he bought three McMuffins, two large fries, and two Dr. Peppers. He popped the oldies tape with the music from the 50's and

6O's into the dash. It was a tape he'd bought the night before because it reminded him of Catlin, and not because Catlin seemed to like the oldies, but more so because he thought she fit more into the fifties' scene than the hip new generation of the 2000's. There was also the fact that he like his dad enjoyed the Beatles, and Elvis, and Rick Nelson. He sometimes told his mother that he wished he had been born fifty years earlier.

It was exactly 7:55 A.M. as he approached Roosevelt Blvd and the light was turning from green to yellow and then to red as he came to a full stop.

Catlin saw him and smiled because she knew in her heart that he was there to offer her a ride to school. Her dress was old fashioned with a full set of underskirts. The red was deep as blood and offset with a bright white belt. It had two solid white string straps allowing her bare shoulders to get an early tan from Florida's famous early warmth and sun.

She even wore Bobby socks that were also white with blood red shoes.

As Randy, ever the old-fashioned gentlemen that both his mother and father taught him to be, reached over the passenger seat and opened the side door.

Getting in the car, there came a breeze from the open door. It carried Catlin's scent to Randy's nostrils and her scent became permanently

11

embedded in his brain cells. A scent he was sure he would be able to pick out of a thousand women were they ever lined up before him.

Catlin pulled the door closed and had a little trouble getting her seat belt to buckle and Randy gladly assisted her.

"I hope you're hungry," he told her offering her an Egg McMuffin, a fry and one of the two medium Dr. Peppers. They ate in silence as he kept to the business of driving the car. He dared to ask her about her boyfriend who he had looked up in the schools' registrar. The only person in the computer with that name had graduated back in 1964.

Randy liked the shyness Catlin seemed to be showing and he asked, "Are you always so quiet?"

She smiled at him as she took a small bite out of her breakfast Mac.

"Are you going to the Prom?" Randy asked as the car rounded the corner to Lee High.

"Are you asking?" Catlin asked him with a smile.

"Yeah, but you mentioned Bobby Bargin as being your boyfriend, and I don't wanna spoil things for you with him," Randy went on to say, "but yeah, if he can't take you, I'd love to. I mean, we've only known each other a few days and all."

Before Randy could react, Catlin reached over and kissed him on the cheek and whispered, "Yes, Randy, I'll go with you to the prom."

"What time do you want me to pick you up and what colors are you wearing?"

Catlin told him "I'll be wearing something like a light green on white."

"Well, I guess I can pick you up about 4:30 P.M. and we can have dinner, take in the dance and see where the night takes us. I can change the color of my cummerbund to match your colors," he told her.

Randy's heart jumped a few beats and he found himself grinning like a Cheshire Cat, then, realizing that he was, swallowed his grin and pulled in the school's parking lot.

"Can I give you a ride home after school, I'd like to meet your parents?" he asked her.

"I'll meet you here after my last class," she promised.

"Deal!" he said as he reached over to hit the button to bring the rag-top up.

Before getting out of the car, Catlin helped him to latch the top into place then did her disappearing act into a passing crowd of students waving bye to him as he locked the car up and grabbed his load of books and headed for his homeroom.

After his last full class of the day, Randy headed for the car. Upon arriving in the student parking lot, he found Catlin standing next to his car.

"Hello, there," he said with a wide grin. "Been here long?"

"Only a few minutes," she answered as he popped the locks on both sides with his remote.

Before he could reach around her to open the car door for her, she opened it and got in and buckled her seatbelt. Going around the car, he got in and followed suit, placing both of their books on the back seat.

"Are you hungry? We could go by Micky D's for a snack. I don't have to work this weekend."

"Okay," she said and they drove off.

As they drove out of the school parking lot, Randy hit his forehead with his right open palm of his hand saying, "Darn, I've got to stop by the cleaners for mom. Do you mind?

"Mom and dad are going out to dinner tonight and I promised I'd pick up her dress and get it straight to her after school."

"It's okay, I don't have any plans anyway," she answered him with a warm smile.

"It'll only take a few minutes, I promise," he told her as he turned onto College Street and headed for a small cleaners on King Street.

Parking at the curb on King, Randy got out leaving the motor running so Catlin could enjoy the cool air of the a/c unit since he'd left the top up. "I'll only be a sec," he told her and walked briskly into the little cleaners.

Taking out the ticket stub his mother gave him, he handed it over, got not only the dress, but a suit his father forgot to pick up the week before.

Returning to the car, he opened his door, pushed back the front seat and hung both garments on the hook that was attached to the roof of the car, then pulled the driver's seat back into place and got in, fastening his seatbelt.

"Thanks," he said, "Mom would have shot me if I'd forgotten." Checking the street for traffic, they pulled away from the curb and made a right on Dartmouth heading for Roosevelt.

Catlin turned on the car radio, picking up WAPE, her favorite oldies station and both sang as "Teen Angel" came on. When the song was over, Randy reached over and opened the glove box and pulled out the tape he bought two days before. Getting it open, he slid it into the tape deck player saying, "I bought this the other night and thought you'd enjoy it."

Elvis was first with "Teddy Bear" and as they drove on the time seemed to fly and the next thing either could remember was turning left into Randy's driveway.

"Come on in, Mom would love to meet you," Randy told her as he opened the car door and retrieved the clothes from the back seat.

"Well," she started to say when Randy opened her door for her. She never had a chance to say no as Randy took her by the hand heading the two of them towards the front door of the house.

Opening the door, Randy handed both garments to Catlin as he opened the door to a closet and moved everything over to allow for the addition of the clothes being hung on a rack Randy had made room for.

"Mom," Randy called out, and in the blink of an eye, Betty Carr stepped from the kitchen just as Randy was closing the closet door.

"Hi, there, I'm glad you didn't forget," Betty told her son, then said, "Hello," to her son's guest.

"Mom, this is Catlin Hyde, she's agreed to go to the prom with me next Friday," he was grinning from ear to ear as he squeezed Catlin's hand.

Catlin just kind of stood there blushing.

"Wow," was about all Betty could utter for the moment.

Taking the girl's hands into her own, she said, "I'm Betty Carr. I'm afraid Randy has been keeping you a secret."

Now it was Randy's turn to blush, and he did. He turned beet red in the face.

Seeing his discomfort, both Betty and Catlin smiled at each other and laughed a little.

"Come on into the kitchen," Betty suggested, still holding onto Catlin's hand guiding her. "I'll get you both a coke and a hot piece of my apple pie. I'll bet you are both starved after a long day in school."

"Mom," Randy started to say, "I told Catlin we'd go to Micky D's" then stopped midsentence and followed them into the kitchen.

Knowing how good her pies were, he was sure Catlin would rather have homemade pie over Micky D's any day, so he just headed to the cupboard and took down three plates and three glasses, placing them on the round kitchen table.

Betty Carr loved the scent of fresh flowers and she had a vase of her favorite ones on the counter she had just trimmed prior to Randy's call. The scent of both fresh baked pie and fresh flowers awed Catlin's senses.

17

"I hope you like apple pie," Randy said. "Mom bakes the best in town," he spoke proudly.

"It's been a long time since I've had any kind of homemade pie, but yes, I love apple," she offered.

Betty opened an air enclosed pie cooler and placed a whole pie on a placemat saying, "I've got some vanilla ice cream in the freezer," nodding towards the large refrigerator and Catlin, and finished by saying, "While I slice up the pie."

Catlin stepped to the frig and started to open the top door, when Randy said, "the freezer is on the bottom."

"Thanks," she said and pulled the door open.

"Top left hand side," Betty told her remembering that she had never been in her kitchen before.

Randy pulled out three forks and the ice cream scoop, handing the scoop to his mother, then the three of them sat down to enjoy their snacks.

Betty, not wanting to embarrass the girl didn't probe too hard. "Are you a senior?" she asked.

"No, ma'am, a junior, I'm afraid," Catlin answered.

Just about the same time they finished eating their pie, Tammy walked in from school. "Hi, everybody," she said with a smile. Then, turning to Catlin, she said, "I'm Tammy," then brought out another plate and glass and sliced herself a piece of pie and sat down.

Getting up, Randy said, "I'd better get you home before your family starts to worry."

"Catlin, it was good to meet you. We hope you'll come back soon," Betty said as she walked the young couple to the door.

"Thank you for the pie and ice cream, it was delicious and I hope to see you again too."

As they walked out the door, Randy kissed his mother on the cheek and said, "I'll be home early. I don't have to work tonight."

"Ready?" Randy asked Catlin.

"Yeah," she replied and then added, "You have a nice family. I'm glad I met them."

Turning on Darcy Street from Roosevelt, Randy pulled over at her house when she said, "Sorry, my mother and father are at work. You can meet them later," then opened the car door and walked up the driveway disappearing between the two houses.

Pulling back onto Roosevelt, Randy made a left on Edgewood, driving

19

down four blocks to Tony's Fine Clothing where he had ordered his tux. He still needed to be fitted. The tailor said it wouldn't take an hour, he already had the appointment and was glad to get it out of the way.

When he got home, it was six fifteen and his family was just sitting down to dinner. An early dinner he reminded himself because his parents were having a late dinner at Ruben's, one of Jacksonville's finest diners. Reservations took a full week, just to get to the front doors.

Brad Thompson, Randy Carr's senior partner had set the all too expensive dinner as a gift to the Carr's for ten years of hard work. Brad had done this every two years since Brad took Randy into their business.

Randy and Betty would reciprocate over New Years at Franklin's on Duval Street, because it was Sandi Thompson's favorite spot.

"Where did you meet Catlin?" Betty asked her son.

"Waiting for her boyfriend at a school bus stop last week," he told her.

"Do what?" Tammy said.

"She was waiting for her boyfriend at the school bus stop to take her to Lee and I offered her a ride," Randy told them.

Frances said, "Hey, that's pretty cool."

"Mom," Nancy asked, "if some good looking boy asked me to ride to school with him, is it alright?"

"No!" Both Randy and his dad said in unison.

"Why not? Randy picked up a strange girl, didn't he?" she persisted.

"Please, listen to me," their mother said. "Hitching a ride is very dangerous! Kids die every day because they didn't know who was who.

"Besides, Catlin probably saw Randy at school and one of her girlfriends told her he was a safe person to ride with," Betty tried to explain.

Randy, knowing his mother was right and was trying to make a strong point on safety with his sisters readily agreed by saying, "That's right, she told me she knew me from school," he lied, but he felt for a good reason.

"Anyway," Randy Senior said flatly. "No one in this house will ever get into another person's car without your mother's and my permission! Is that clear?"

Everyone clearly understood and agreed.

"Well," said Tammy, "what about Randy picking up a stranger?"

That goes for picking anyone up in your car, too!" Randy told his namesake, then added, "Catlin is your only exception."

Tammy smiled and the matter was dropped.

Saturday morning began just after their parents returned from one of their most memorable nights out in many a year, "We danced," his mother told him, "until 4 o'clock, and we ate foods that I'd only heard about, but more than any of that, we had time to explore each other again. And speaking for myself, I think I like your father and if he is good, I might even keep him around for another twenty years or so," she said with a knowing smile for the love of her life.

"I'll make us some breakfast," Betty told her sleepy headed son and husband.

Scrambled eggs and thick slices of bacon were soon being dished out as Randy Jr. did the English Muffins, his dad did the OJ and within ten minutes the three of them were eating a quiet meal.

"What's your schedule, Son?" Randy asked.

"I'm afraid it's gonna be a long weekend for me," he explained. "We've got a client being sued over an accident that could cost him his entire business, not to mention his life savings," Randy concluded.

"Mr. Smith called last night and said he feels we can build a strong defense, and he is counting on us to build it. We've each got an idea where we're gonna explore today, and put our heads together tomorrow and let the boss choose the direction he wants us to pursue," he told them.

"I'm glad I didn't take Law," his father told him. "You have to put in way too many hours to be able to enjoy life."

"Well, I enjoy the challenge and the long hours won't last much past this summer. Besides, I start college in July so I can pick up some extra credits," he reminded his parents.

"Randy," his mother spoke up, "These long hours you speak of are keeping you from getting the rest you'll need throughout college. And, Son, you are wrong on one count already."

"What's that, Mom?" he asked.

"As a Law Clerk," she said, "which is what you will be all through your college years, you will continue to work long and even longer hours until you pass the Bar Exam, and with that, you are still looking at four to six long, tiresome years. And, not to mention, that most attorneys fail the Bar Exam several times before they pass."

"Do you think Catlin, or any girl, is gonna put up with and be willing to wait up all hours of the night just to fix you a hot meal?"

"Son, I'm not trying to dissuade you, but if you really like Catlin, you've got to start taking her and her feelings and needs into consideration, especially about the long, lonely future she will have, whether it's for the next four years, or the next twenty. Remember, Son, she has feelings and needs, too."

This was the first really serious discussion Randy had ever had with his parents, and yes, he had much more on his plate to take into consideration than he was up till now even willing to think about.

"Mom, Dad, you are both right," he said quietly as he finished his breakfast and started to clean off the table, placing the dirty dishes in the dishwasher.

"I guess I hadn't really taken anybody else's feelings and needs into consideration, but I promise you this much, I will."

Randy made his excuses and said, "Right now, I've got to get going, I promised the gang I'd bring the donuts from Dunkin on my way in, and I'm supposed to be there by 6:30."

"Well," his father said, "So long as you don't do all your heavy thinking behind the wheel of the car."

Laughing, he said, "I got the message, Dad."

While at work, Randy gave a lot of thought to what his parents had said and the wisdom in their words asking, "Hey, Wendy," a co-senior

24

at Lee who had helped him land his job, he asked, "Do you have much of a social life, or is it just school and work?"

"What's wrong with school and work? It's enough for me for the moment," the eighteen year old blonde answered, but avoided the real question until Randy pointed it out for her.

"No; I mean not being able to spend time with Steve, like he might want you to," Randy asked again.

"What's Steve got to do with school and my job?" Wendy asked.

"I'm talking about your time together," Randy explained. "I mean with all the time we spend in school plus the long hours we put in here. Does he ever complain about wanting to spend more time with you than what you are able to give?"

"Yeah," Wendy said, "We argue all the time about our all-nighters and I complain about being tired, and he just doesn't understand that this job is very important to me and my future.

"Then he complains about how tired and irritable I am all week and after school, but then again, my mother complains about the same things and throws in that I don't clean up after myself anymore, I mean, like, I ever did. They both say I work too hard, and don't remember that I have a family."

It wasn't too hard for Randy to see just where he had almost lost it all,

25

and said, "I guess we all do work too many hours," then added, "I met this really great girl from Lee two weeks ago, and I'd really like to spend more than forty-five minutes a day with her.

"Dad says that I'll lose her if I don't cut down on my hours, and mom feels that Catlin is a very special girl. I've got to agree, she really stole my heart the first day I laid eyes on her," Randy told his friend.

It's hard to believe you actually found a girlfriend," Wendy told her best bud.

"Are you taking her to the prom next week?" Wendy asked.

"I don't know as you could call her my girlfriend," he replied. "The day I met her, she told me up-front she had a boyfriend named Bobby Bargin and that he was a senior at Lee. I couldn't find his name in the school registrar.

"The only Bobby Bargin I found graduated from Lee in 1964. I guess her boyfriend must be his son," Randy went on. "When I mentioned the prom earlier this week, she seemed interested and even asked if I was asking. I was dumbfounded at first, and jumped when she said yes, but I told her I didn't want to get between her and her boyfriend. Then she just smiled and reached over and kissed me saying "Yes, I'll go to the prom with you. She never mentioned Bobby again," Randy told her.

"Yesterday, I took her home to meet my mother. Mom told dad she thought Catlin was beautiful and conservative in her dress and make-up. I guess she likes her almost as much as I do," he said.

"It sounds to me as though you've got yourself a real live girlfriend," Wendy told him, then said, "if we don't get this case started, we both might find ourselves with all too much time on our hands after the boss fires us."

Chapter 2

He sees the beauty
That existed then
Now only a silhouette
Through a lightened gown.

Monday morning came all too early for Randy. He didn't get woke up by his mother until 6:15 when she presented him with fried eggs, scattered new potatoes, fresh OJ, and toast with his favorite strawberry jam on a platter with a steaming hot cup of coffee in bed.

"You stay there," she instructed him. "You can miss a day of school. I won't have you climbing behind the wheel of your car just to fall asleep getting yourself killed when you don't have to."

As tired as he was, he couldn't argue with her. He ate two bites of his breakfast and was fast asleep within seconds. His mother walking by a few moments later removed the tray and went back down stairs and ate the breakfast her all-too-sleepy son didn't.

It was 7:20 when Randy woke with a start. He jumped out of bed and literally ran out of the house half dressed; pulling on a pair of Nikes as he headed for his car. He had barely cleared the driveway when his cell phone went off. He had made a promise not to talk on the cell phone when driving, so he looked at it at the first stoplight, seeing it was his mother, he pulled to the curb and called her back.

"What in the world was that all about, Randy?"

"Mom, I forgot, I promised Catlin I'd pick her up this morning. I don't want someone else picking her up, and I never asked her for her phone number, so forgive me, but I had to go," he explained.

"Son, you darn near scared me out of my wits. You should have said something. I would have picked her up for you," Betty told him.

"As tired as I was, and still am, I didn't think about that. Sorry!" he told her sounding very serious. "I'll remember to get her number so we can have it on hand, okay? Maybe I can talk her into skipping school and then we can spend a little time together, if you don't mind," he suggested.

"If it won't get her into trouble; check with her parents first, then invite her here for some lunch," Betty said.

"Okay, mom; I've gotta go," Randy begged off. But before he hung up, he said, "Thanks, Mom. Love ya!" then folded the phone and pulled away from the curb. The time was 7:37 A.M.

Randy didn't have time to stop and pick up something to eat, but he pulled to a stop at exactly 7:55 at the corner of Edgewood and

Roosevelt Boulevard It was no surprise that Catlin was already there.

"Hey, there," Randy said through the window.

"Good morning to you, too," Catlin said as she quickly climbed into the car. Then looking at him asked, "What in the world happened to you? You look like something even the cat might not want to drag in." Then kissed him on the cheek.

"It's been a long, long weekend at work. Our boss has us going over old case files looking for an edge in a case going to court in two weeks. We started Saturday morning and darn near worked straight through until 1:30 this morning. So I feel about as dead as I look," he told her.

"Can't you skip a day or two to rest up a little?" she asked.

"Mom said I could take today off and she'd cover for me, but I don't feel like sleeping all day, it'll only make me more tired. I was hoping to talk you into skipping class too so we could spend the day together, but mom said not to get you in any trouble," he said.

"You know what my mother would say if I approached her?" she asked.

"No, but I can guess it would go something like this – 'Catlin, you hardly know the boy!' No, we'd better not ask, it might put me in a bad light with them."

31

"Hmm," she said. "You really don't know my mother! What she'd say is "If he is working that hard to build a future and still going to school, a day off once in awhile is a worthy reward. Then she'd tell me if you want to spend the day off with him, I'd certainly say okay. And that's what my mom would say," she told him.

"Wow! Really? I mean even without knowing anything otherwise about me. But, my mother said to ask first. So we'd better."

"I would expect both mom and dad are gonna be out until after this afternoon and there is no way to reach either of them. "I'm sure they'd both agree," she assured him.

"Are you sure?" he asked.

"Yes, Randy, I'm sure it'll be okay. Besides, spending a whole day with you will be nice," Catlin smiled assuringly and then added, "What do you want to do first?"

"EAT!" was his answer. "I sure hope you're hungry," he smiled back at her.

"I feel like I haven't eaten a decent meal in fifty years," she told him.

"We could go home, Mom would love to cook breakfast for us," Randy said. "Or, we could go to Denny's for a Grand Slam."

"Well," Catlin said, "I don't know what a 'Grand Slam' is, but I do like your mother, and being around a family would really make me feel alive again."

Randy thought to himself, "*What a strange way to put it,*" then let it go as they headed back to Randy's house. It was just past 8:15 as they walked in the front door.

"Mom!" Randy called out.

"Hey, you two," Betty said as she came down the stairs.

"Good morning, Mrs. Carr," Catlin said with a smile.

"Catlin," Betty said. "My name is Betty, you don't have to call me Mrs. Carr," she said, "After all, I'm not his grandmother '

"Yes, ma'am," Catlin relented.

Taking both of Catlin's hands into her own, Betty got a good look at her sleepy-headed son who had the dark shadow of a fast growing and thick blonde beard and suggested, "Randy, why don't I take Catlin to the kitchen while you get yourself a shower and a shave?"

Running his hand over his rough face, Randy said, "I'll be down in a few minutes. Mom is right; I do need a shower and a shave, even if I am slumming today," then he excused himself. Taking the stairs two at a time, he disappeared somewhere at the top.

"Come on, I'll fix us some juice and coffee," Betty told her. Without another word, they headed for the kitchen.

Entering the warm kitchen, Catlin headed straight for the frig. There, she took out a nearly full pitcher of OJ, taking it to the round table the Carr's ate on when not using the formal dining room. The dining room separated the kitchen from the living room.

Catlin picked up the glass vase of brightly colored flowers and said, "These are all different. Some are spring flowers, some are from the summer, and yet you have them fresh. Even these fall season flowers look fresh like they've just been picked. How can a full years worth of fresh cut flowers be found in one vase? I've never seen or smelled such beauty," she told her hostess.

"Thank you for the compliment," Betty told her. "I've found several florists in the area that can bring in flowers from around the world, so when it's in the dead of winter here, fresh roses and carnations with many others are just going into bloom in Chile and Mexico. They import them for us," she explained.

"Well, they're lovely and their scents are to die for," Catlin said honestly.

Laughing, Betty replied, "They are nice, but I don't know as if I'd go so far as to die for them. Although, they do make the house smell nice, and besides, they do brighten up the kitchen," she finished.

34

"What can I do to help?" Catlin asked.

"Grab the eggs and bacon out of the frig, I'll peel some potatoes," Betty suggested.

As Catlin was getting the eggs and bacon, she also took some cheese, placing it on the counter near the stove. "Where can I find the frying pan and the mixing bowl?"

"There," Betty said pointing to a lower cabinet in the rear corner opposite the frig.

"Randy is very tired," Catlin told Betty.

"I know; he's too pale. He needs to get out and soak up some sun," Betty offered.

"It's gonna be a beautiful day, and it's going to get hot later in the day. I wish I could get him to the beach. He loves the waves and the salt water," Betty shared with her.

"I could talk him into taking me to the beach, but I don't have a bathing suit," Catlin said.

"Hey, that's a great idea. I think he'd go for it if you brought it up, and I'm sure I can find one of my suits that'll fit you," Betty said with a warm smile as she thought to herself, "*I don't know where you came from but I hope you stick around for a long time!*"

By the time the potatoes were peeled and Catlin, who had donned one of Betty's kitchen aprons, was breaking a dozen eggs into a mixing bowl Randy came in dressed in jeans and a polo shirt. "Hey, Catlin, how would you like to spend the day out in the sun?"

The heads of the two women came up and looked at each other as Catlin answered, "I don't know. What do you have in mind?"

"I was thinking about a full day at the beach soaking up some rays. We could go by your house and pick up a bathing suit then hit the KFC for some fried chicken," Randy suggested.

Looking at each other, Betty said with a shrug, "Sounds like a plan to me."

"Randy, I don't have a bathing suit," Catlin answered, not telling him that his mother had already offered her the use of one of hers.

Catlin was cooking home fries in the frying pan when the waft of the cooking hit Randy. "Hmm, that smells good. I didn't know you could cook."

"Look at me," Catlin said stopping Randy in his tracks as he indeed did look at her.

Betty, seeing her son in a different light giggled and said to Catlin, "I think he is taking a good look at you and likes what he is seeing." Then she said, "Okay you two stop it. You can goggle at each other when you're at the beach, and I think I've got just the bathing suit to fit you and the mood, Catlin," Betty said to change the mood as they prepared the table. "What are you wearing to the prom?"

"I had a very special gown made that has many layers of soft lime with layers of white lace and pink silk with a matching pair of shoes, and a ribbon to wear in my hair. The belt is wide with a hidden buckle under an eightinch, multi-layered sash of pure pink silk with white lace," Catlin told them.

"Wow!" Randy exclaimed. "Those are nearly the same colors I ordered for my tux. My pants and jacket are white with light green stripes on the outer legs, and a matching green silk shirt with a royal pink cummerbund with black shoes."

Betty was floored! Then, she went to the refrigerator and pulled out two cartons. One containing a bright red carnation. The other a mixed color of red, and pink and cream corsage and laid them both on the table before the two youngsters.

"They're," Catlin started to say as Randy joined in with, "They're beautiful, Mom! How did you know what colors to get?"

"I didn't really," she explained. "These were the last two of alike colors anyone had left. It was these or plain white or red."

"They really are beautiful, Mrs. Carr. Do you think they'll last until the weekend?" Catlin asked.

"Oh, they'll last much longer than that," she told them. "When you get home after the prom, put it back into its box and back into the refrigerator and you'll have it to wear during your dinner after graduation or in this case, after Randy's graduation." Then she took both flowers and put them back in the frig and said, "When Randy picks you up, ya'll stop by here and I'll pin them on you and take a few pictures."

"Deal!" Randy said as he finished eating.

While Randy cleared the dishes, his mother took Catlin up to her bedroom where she found some swimsuits and placed them on the bed. "I found three suits that should fit you," Betty said. "Why don't you take them into the bathroom and try them on."

Catlin found she had three to choose between a dark blue one piece, a red background two piece with small white dots, and a pale green bikini, that seemed way too small to her eyes, but she was willing to try on all three as instructed to by Betty.

Trying on the polka dot one first, she quickly took it off – it was too small for her. Next, she tried on the one piece blue and went back into the bedroom where Betty had her turn around and said, "It's nice on you, but why don't you try one of the two piece suits. I think either will suit your youthful figure."

Returning to the bathroom, she put the polka dot suit back on and came out for Betty to see.

"Now, that's more like it, but the dots don't fit your personality. Try on the green one, it might be little, but it might be just what the Doctor ordered."

Going back into the bathroom, Catlin slipped out of the polka dots and stepped into the little green one, and pulled it into place, then returned to the bedroom where Betty waited.

Standing there, waiting for Betty to say something, Catlin felt a little out of sorts until Betty finally said, "Turn around slowly."

Turning as instructed, she soon began to feel self-conscience when Betty said, "I think this is the one. It is certainly better on you than it ever was on me; fits your personality better than it did mine, too."

Walking over to the full length mirror, Catlin had a chance to see what Betty was seeing. "Not bad!" she said smiling. Do you think Randy will like it?"

"Personally speaking," Betty told her, "I think you'd look great in any of them, but this one, he'll love. You'll knock Randy's socks off when he sees you."

"Well, I'd better not let him see me until after we get there," Catlin said jokingly. "I don't want his mind on anything else until we park the car."

Serious now, Betty looked again at the young woman and said, "You seem to know Randy a little better than I thought you would."

"No, not really, but I do know boys and how distracted they can get when they see a girl in a bathing suit," Catlin joked.

"Now there is something we both can agree on," Betty said and they both laughed.

"You'd better keep it on. There won't be any place to change when you get there," Betty told her.

After putting the other two suits away, Betty handed Catlin a pair of cut off jeans and a pull over sleeveless top to wear, a pair of flip flops and handed her a gym bag to put her clothes in. "We'd better find you some Coppertone Sunscreen. You're as pale as Randy," and handed her a pair of sun glasses then suggested they go to the linen closet for a couple of beach towels and half a dozen towels to dry off with and to sit on once they got back into Randy's car.

"Come on," Betty told her as they headed back down stairs.

Randy had just come out of the pantry carrying a white box.

"Look what I found," he told his mother, then he stopped dead in his tracks as he saw Catlin descending the final step. "WOW," was about all he got out as Catlin walked straight up to him and planted a kiss on his lips. It wasn't a passionate kiss, per se, but it was enough to shut Randy up before he could say much of anything else.

"Great," Betty said, "You found the igloo. You can pick up some ice at the Seven-Eleven on your way."

The kiss wasn't missed and she smiled to herself thinking, "The more I see of this girl, the more I like her."

"Randy," Betty suggested, "why don't you run upstairs and find your bathing suit. We'll get things together down here. You'll have to pick up some suntan lotion when you pick up the ice. The bottle we have is two years old and might not be any good."

"I'll remember," he assured his mother as he hit the stairway.

"I think this is gonna be fun," Catlin said. "It's been a lifetime since I had a full day out."

"I hope you don't get into trouble over it," Betty told her.

"No, I think I can get away with it this one time, and even if I get grounded, it will have been worth it," Catlin said smiling at her from her seat.

"Well, if you do get in trouble over it, have your folks call me. I'll explain that it was all my idea," Betty suggested.

Then Catlin bent over and hugged and kissed Betty on the cheek, and said, "Thank you. This will be a day I'll remember for all times."

Looking into the pantry, Betty found some cookies and some granola bars and handed them to Catlin saying, "Put these in the cooler for later" then had a thought. "Do you like fresh fruit?"

"Yes, ma'am," she answered.

"Good," Betty said. "Why don't ya'll stop by the Food Fair and pick up some at the deli. It's already cut and diced in trays and Randy never gets enough fresh fruit with all the crazy hours he puts in at that law firm. It will do you both some good as the day wears on."

"I'll tell him," Catlin promised.

Betty suddenly had thoughts of scenes like this happening many times in the future with each of her children and grandchildren and wondered where all the time had gone. Had it really been nineteen years since she had gotten married?

The thought passed in the blink of an eye and her son met them in the kitchen where Catlin asked him, "Did you do the dishes already?"

"Yeah, I rinsed them and put them in the dishwasher," he told her.

"Dishwasher?" she said questioning him.

'Yeah, the dishwasher!" he said as he opened the machine and showed her.

Laughing, she said "I was always the dishwasher at home. I hope I can have one of those when I get married."

"Every new house and most older homes have dishwashers these days. Where have you been for the last fifty years, hiding your head in a hole in the ground?" Randy asked jokingly.

"In a manner of speaking," Catlin answered.

"If we're going," Randy said, "we'd best hit the road." Then kissed his mother and said, "Don't hold dinner, we might be out late."

"Just drive carefully," his mother admonished as she kissed Catlin on the cheek.

"Bye!" all three said as they headed for the door.

℘

Chapter 3

She was once loved
Then taken away
Leaving behind her soul
To a saddened heart

After stopping at the Seven-Eleven for ice and bottled water, Catlin remembered her promise to Betty to have Randy stop by the Food Fair's deli for some fresh fruit and she informed Randy as they had just crossed the St. Mathews Bridge.

"We'll stop here at the Town & Country Shopping Center which is in Arlington, and get what we need," he suggested.

Getting out of the car at the shopping center, Catlin wanted to remain in the car, but Randy talked her into going with him.

Entering the large, spacious store, the fluorescent lighting brought out the bright coloring of each item they encountered. Vegetables were greener, milk was more white than it's normal cream coloring. Even the price tags seemed brighter and friendlier, even if the prices seemed to Catlin to be outrageous.

I can't believe the prices of everything," Catlin told Randy as they rounded another aisle.

"Yeah," he agreed, not knowing exactly what she meant but said in a word, "Inflation!"

The aisle in front of them was the deli, Catlin acted like a small child in a candy store for the first time looking and pointing out one item after another.

"Haven't you ever been to the grocery store before?" Randy teased her.

"Yes, but it's seems like it was fifty years ago, or in another lifetime," she told him.

"What a strange thing for a seventeen year old to say," Randy thought to himself, as she stepped down the counter aisle from him. Then another strange thing happened. Randy must have been fifteen feet away from Catlin when he happened to glance indirectly towards her. Her body seemed translucent and even her silhouette shimmered. *"Am I really looking right through her? It must be a trick of the lights,"* he said to himself.

He took another look, only this time a hard and direct look. He had heard of mirages and the likes but he could clearly see those things behind her and then the seeming illusion vanished as she walked towards him saying with mirth, "Are you looking at me or through

46

me?" And then kissed him.

"This can't be real," he thought to himself. *"I've only known her for two weeks, yet it seems like I've known her all our lives. I've never even had a girlfriend, at least not a real girlfriend, and wow, look at her, she really likes me. Well, in a way."*

"I was just thinking how lucky I am that you wanted to spend the day with me," Randy told her as she kissed him again. *"Boy, could I get used to this!"* his thoughts continued.

After buying some fruit and Gatorade and a few more bottles of fresh spring water, they started to leave when Randy remembered that the sun screen his mother gave them was two years old and nearly empty, and he headed them towards the drugs when Catlin saw some beach towels and clear rubber inner tubes and some swim suits.

"Now," Randy thought to himself, *"what girl could refuse a little shoping spree,"* as she made a beeline straight to the two piece bikinis.

Holding up one suit to her front, then another, she asked, "What do you think?"

"I think I'm about to be reminded why I want and need to become an attorney," and they both laughed.

They spent the next half hour as Catlin tried on four different swim suits, and decided that she and Randy liked the one his mother had loaned her the best. However, they did pick out a pair of sun glasses and a Mexican sombrero she thought she'd wear in the sun, and a white scarf to tie it down with. They also picked up a bottle of Coppertone 35 and she asked him, "I don't remember seeing all these numbers before. What are they for?"

"Let's say," he started, "that you are Mexican or a real American Indian who lived in the West or Midwest and that you were used to living in the sun. Your skin would be used to its rays, then you wouldn't need such a high number. Then there are people like us 'pale-faces' that only get in the sun once or twice a year. Our skin is very sensitive to the sun's rays and can cause us to get sunburned which can cause skin cancer, so what we need at the beginning of summer is a very high number to help us tan and not burn. So, I choose the highest number they have, which is currently 35, but I suspect it might go much higher by next year, might even reach as high as fifty," he finished.

Once they were done paying, they headed for the car where Randy put everything into either the gym bag or the cooler and then put the top down again.

Catlin said, "Everything is so automatic, a person today has only to push a button, or read about what's best to use. Heck," she said, "you don't even have to cook, just buy things daily from a store like this and you won't even have pots and pans to wash."

Then she said another quirky thing Randy thought odd as she asked, "I noticed that you used one of those plastic cards to pay for gas for the car, another at the store. Don't people use money anymore?"

"Catlin," Randy said, "Credit cards have been around for nearly forty years, you know that," and he added, "Debit Cards are the 'in' thing these days, where the price of your purchase comes directly out of your checking or savings account at the bank." Then concluded with, "Where have you been hiding?"

"Wow, you're making fun of me," she said frowning.

Sometimes, it's best to keep ones mouth shut, Randy remembered his father saying one day, and decided that this must be one of those times and he said seriously, "I'm sorry, I didn't mean to tease you."

The top was down; it was close to 11am. The warm wind was blowing her hair; she put a smile on her face and took the tape out of the glove box and put it in the dash and turned the music on a little louder and began to sing along with Elvis.

Her voice was musical and magical; both clear and strong.

She poked Randy in the side and teased him into singing along with her. The sour mood of the past moment forgotten as they both got into the music doing fifty-five miles an hour heading for a fun-filled day at the beach.

They passed the Regency Mall and where Atlantic blended into Beach Blvd the traffic thinned out and they sang along with the Everly Brothers, Ricky Nelson, and the Beach Boys as the beach quickly began to take form before them. The twenty-two mile stretch was gone in the blink of an eye.

Randy drove past Pacific Avenue and route A1A then followed Beach Boulevard as it ended at the oceans tide. The tide was high but all along Jacksonville Beach there was at least five hundred feet of firm sand.

Florida beaches are different than most other beaches along the east coast because you can drive on the hard packed sand and it doesn't shift when you stop or park your car for long periods of time.

Randy's father, while stationed in Jacksonville, North Carolina back in 1985, had taken his mother to the beach and had parked their car as they would have in Florida, only in North Carolina. The sand began to shift while they were in swimming and playing in the surf, and within half an hour, their car was carried out to the water's edge, and by the time he had retrieved the keys from the area they had spread the beach blanket, which was now more than several hundred feet away, the front of the car was already covered with water. It was a lesson his father shared with the entire family over the years.

"Let's go down by Neptune Beach, there'll be less people and we can turn the radio up," Randy suggested and turned the car south.

Catlin was absorbed in all the activities going on around her. The Boardwalk with its big Ferris wheel that had teams of people crawling all over it, "What are they doing?" she asked of no one.

Being the only one around who could have heard her question Randy answered with, "I think they're changing the lights and doing repairs," as they continued to drive down the beach front.

As the young couple drove out of the small business district, Catlin saw dozens of recently built apartment, and several hotels along the beach front, but they too soon thinned out leaving a smatter of older homes. Some were very close to the water front; others were set back several thousand feet. Those houses each had a wooden walkway leading from the houses down through the dunes to the beaches hard surfaces of the sand.

When the last of the houses were left behind them, Catlin noticed a large curvature in the makeup of the beach itself as it curved inward like to a cove, but not so deep or pronounced but definitely noticeable when Randy suggested, "This is the northern most part of Neptune Beach. The main beach traffic is several miles south of here. Let's look for a safe area to park."

Pointing, Catlin put her left hand on Randy's arm and said, "This area looks good. What do you think?"

Looking where she had pointed, he saw a trash barrel mounted on what appeared to be railroad ties buried deep in the sand and painted red, white and blue. The barrel had a solid white sign with black lettering he still couldn't read, but thought it was to remind the beach goers not to litter.

Randy pulled the car as close to the dunes as he could, then the two of them took out the large beach blanket his mother gave them to use and since the tide was already at its highest point, they placed the blanket between the car and the water's edge some fifty feet away.

It wasn't long after their arrival that the two were splashing at the water's edge.

"I can't go any deeper," Catlin told him.

"Why not, can't you swim? The waters not too rough."

Kicking water at him she said, "No. Bobby was gonna teach me, but I haven't seen him in a long time and no one else has been around to teach me," Catlin told him.

"The water's calm and I'm here. Come on, we won't go too deep, and I'll teach you at least enough to save your life," Randy told her as he took her hand pulling her out to where the water was closer to waist high.

The waves rolled gently by them as he first showed Catlin how to float on her back saying "The main thing about floating is not to panic. Floating is very relaxing and easy to do, and can give you back much of your energies you use to swim with it, so if you get too tired to swim while swimming, just turn over on your back and allow yourself to float."

Randy had both of his hands under Catlin's back as she tried doing what he had shown her.

"This isn't so hard," she laughed. It was the perfect time for a much larger wave to break not three feet behind her head. It caught them both by surprise, giving each a mouth and nose full of salty foam.

Turning over quickly, Caitlin fought to get her feet back on solid ground. She felt lucky as Randy took hold of her, righting her and drawing her close to his own body as they both held on to each other for what seemed an eternity.

Randy hadn't considered how close Catlin was to him until he suddenly felt her wet skin in almost total contact with his own. Their arms were tightly around each other when Catlin looked up and kissed him as she whispered, "Thank you. You saved me."

Then she pushed away from him heading towards shore. With each step she took, she splashed Randy with a stream of water, laughing and kicking the entire way.

Taking off after her in the same playful manner, Randy punched wave after wave at her until his feet could do more damage by kicking than his fist could do by punching at the warm, salty foam of the ocean.

Exiting the surf, they both danced the craziness of the moment dance, half walking like a drunkard; first, forward a few steps then from side-to-side with half steps backwards until they reached the safety of the soft dry sands of the flat part of the outer dune where they had spread the beach blanket.

Reaching for a clean towel out of the gym bag, Catlin vigorously dried her hair while Randy, who didn't mind being wet, opened the cooler and took out two pints of Glacier Clear Water, opening one bottle and handing it to Catlin, then opened one for himself and took a deep pull of the cooling fluid.

It was then that Randy remembered the sun-screen lotion, and took the new bottle of Coppertone out and said "Hey, before we both burn to a cinder, we'd better get some lotion on us."

"Do you want me to put some on your back?" he asked.

"Thank you" she said as she sat down pulling her legs up and leaning forward towards her knees. Then she untied the strap to the top of her bathing suit, pulled her long hair to one side exposing the nape of her neck that had a raspberry the size of a dime dead center and just below her hairline.

Sitting down directly behind her, his legs straddling her, he first used a little water from his bottle to rinse his hands, then put a large dab of lotion in his hands and rubbed them together.

When he was sure his hands were clean and warm, he put several droplets on her shoulders and another dab on her neck, then began to work the Coppertone into her already hot skin.

Being a virgin, Randy had never been this close to a girl other than his two sisters who never untied their upper straps.

Slowly Randy worked the lotion down her back going from side-to-side rubbing in small circles until his hands came close to her breast. It was at that point that Catlin chose to sit upright suddenly, catching Randy unprepared and both of his hands cupped her taunt breast.

Freezing his motion, Randy started to apologize when Catlin moved her face towards his, kissed him and placed his hands back on her breasts and nipples and from there, Mother Nature took over.

An hour later after exploring all that each had to offer, both young people lay spent and covered only with a wide beach towel.

Catlin said, "I'm starved, let's eat some fruit," as she unabashedly slipped out of Randy's embrace and reached towards the cooler totally naked and took out the two trays of fruit they had bought.

During the next hour, Catlin hand fed Randy one piece of melon after

55

another, allowing her fingers to be licked and sucked on by him. Then it was his turn to tease her and she took well advantage of his offerings. Two hours later, spent again and since there still hadn't been a single car go by, Catlin didn't say a single word as she took Randy by the hand and led him back into the warm beach water, leaving both bathing suits on the blanket.

Randy had never been skinny dipping but after feeling the freedom he felt wasn't so sure he wouldn't want to do this again.

Randy decided he'd try again to teach Catlin a little more about how to swim. "Lay flat on my hands," he told her. "I won't let another wave overtake us. Now, stretch your arms out over your head and cup your hands," he instructed her.

It was then he looked at her naked butt sticking out of the water like two islands, and decided that he liked what he saw.

"Now, slowly kick your feet and pull one hand of the water towards you at a time, reaching for another handful with the other."

As she demonstrated the movements for him, he smiled and said. "Don't forget to breathe. You do that by turning your head opposite the arm you are drawing towards your side."

After practicing the movements for a few more minutes, Randy decided that, "We'd better go put some clothes on. Someone is bound to come by and we can't get out if there are people around.**"**

After considering his words of wisdom, she agreed and they walked out almost expecting someone to be watching them.

Once they were decent, Randy suggested they hit the local KFC which he believed was about three miles south. They weren't in any hurry to go anywhere, but both were hungry.

Prior to packing up the car, they shook out the blanket and towels, folded them, and Randy put them in the trunk after taking out fresh bottles of cold water, handing one to Catlin.

"Thank you, kind sir,'" she teased.

Pulling back onto the hard packed beach, they saw not one car coming their way, but several. Looking at each other, both at first grinned then Catlin started to laugh as she told Randy, "I guess we picked the right time to leave," which made both laugh all the harder.

Randy could just imagine the headlines in the Jacksonville Journal the next morning with this caption, "Neptune Beach Turns Nude," showing him and Catlin in bold living color making out or swimming in the nude. Not only would he be arrested for having sex with a minor, but he would lose his job, his car, his scholarship, and his chance to get into law school.

The worst part would be that both would be forever barred from ever seeing the other. At the moment that would be unbearable and none of it was a laughing matter yet both he and Catlin still laughed until they saw a Beach Patrol heading back towards where they had parked nearly five hours before.

"Look at the time," Randy said as they pulled on A1A. "Where did all the time go?"

"Fly times when fun's having you," Catlin said, even if she mixed up the words, it did sound about right.

"Yeah" he said as he grinned and she put her hand on his.

"Are you hungry?" Randy asked again.

"Uh huh, I feel like I haven't eaten in fifty years," she said.

Without thinking about what she might have meant by that, Randy said "Me too!"

"Have you tried their roasted chicken?" Randy asked.

"No, what is roasted chicken? I've never heard of it," she told him.

"It's like smoked chicken," he tried to explain. "It's the best chicken I've ever eaten and not even Popeye's is doing it yet. If you haven't tried it, I think you'll like it."

"Okay," she said. "I'm willing." Then squeezed his hand in a tempting and teasing manner he had never known before which started to arouse him again.

"You better stop teasing me or I'll have to find us a motel," he said seriously.

"Alright," she said with a pout. "Besides, I'm hungrier than I thought." She bent over and kissed him on the cheek.

While they ate roasted chicken, macaroni with cheese, cole slaw and buttermilk biscuits, they talked about school and Randy's work and work schedule. Randy later suggested "You know, it's still early, I'm gonna call mom and tell her I'm taking you to the movies. That way she won't worry. She'll want you to call your mother too, before we both get into trouble," he told her.

"I'll call and leave a message in case they're not home, but they said they'd be gone until after ten or eleven," Catlin agreed.

"Back at the Town & Country Shopping Center, next to the Food Fair, the theater was playing *'Love Story'*, with Ryan O'Neil. I saw it a long time ago and it kinda fits my mood," he told her. Then asked," Have you ever seen it?"

"No," she said "but with a name like 'Love Story', it must be good."

"It was in its day, but I still like it and others like 'Ghost' or 'Sleepless in Seattle," Randy told her.

59

As they finished eating, both made their calls.

Betty Carr insisted that Catlin give her number to her parents in case they were worried or needed to call.

"Okay, mom I'll have her leave both of our numbers for them. We'll be home before eleven."

"Just be careful son and keep your seat belts on," Betty reminded her only son, "And have fun!"

"Thanks, mom; we'll be fine." then hung up and quickly wrote down his phone numbers handing them to Catlin who heard his side of the conversion with his mother.

After he made sure she called and left the numbers, they headed for the movie as the radio played *"Earth Angel"*. When the song finished playing, Randy's Mustang had just pulled to a stop as Catlin took Randy's hand in hers and said, "Let's make that our song."

It seemed very old fashioned, and it was an old fashioned song, much like Catlin and he agreed. This was just another first for him, another of the many that would await his future.

He had a lot to think about since getting his car and a girlfriend. He realized that things were moving much too fast and he needed to find a way to slow things down.

It seemed to Randy that the movie didn't last but fifteen minutes before he found himself behind the wheel of the car heading for home. Catlin, after doing a lot of crying during and after the movie, sat quietly at his side in a subdued mood.

"Hey," he said to her to help lighten the mood, "it was only a movie."

"I know," Catlin said, "but it was based on a true story and after today, it made me do a lot of thinking."

"About us?" he asked.

"Yeah," then they sat quietly for what seemed like days before she spoke again, she waited for the car to catch a stop light so she could have Randy's full attention.

When it became apparent they weren't gonna catch a light and they were going through College Station, Catlin asked if there was some place he could pull over.

"There's a Steak & Shake up ahead on King. We could stop for a soda or a shake," he suggested.

"Okay, but I'm really not thirsty," she told him.

Instead, he pulled into a little strip shopping area at College and George and turned the car off, then turned to face her.

61

The evening was late, there was only a few cars around and fewer people as Catlin unbuckled her belt and turned to face him. "You know," she started, "I had a boyfriend, Bobby, but during the last few weeks, I've learned that I never really loved him."

Randy's heart jumped into his throat as she continued.

"Today was the most special day of my life, and I discovered that I am very much in love with you." Then she reached up taking his face into her hands, pulling his face towards hers and kissed him on the lips gently before settling back down in her seat and putting her seat belt back on.

Randy wasn't too surprised and said, "Up until today, I wasn't sure I even knew what love was; but, after today - and I don't mean the great sex, and it was great - but after thinking about how much my life has changed in such a short time and how much you mean to me, I think I can understand a little more the love between my parents."

"When you see one of them alone, without the other, it is easy to see that a piece of them is missing. It's funny, in a weird way, but I've felt all weekend a loneliness that I couldn't understand until you got into the car this morning. Now, I feel," he paused as he gathered his thoughts and feelings for a few more seconds, and then added, "maybe more complete, but not, not yet fully completed."

"Perhaps that will come with marriage, or having children, I don't know yet." Then he smiled, satisfied with his answers and finished with "We're still young. I've got to get through college, and you've got to finish high school. There is no reason why we should have to make any lifetime decisions tonight. Recognizing our love for one another is a major step and I feel that is in the right direction. Our lives are just now at their beginning, I know that loving you is the single most important thing in my life and I don't know about how you feel right now, but it scares me!"

About all Catlin could say to this news was, "Yeah, I know exactly how you feel. It scares the heck out of me, too."

The rest or the ride to Catlin's house they remained quiet and reserved. When the car stopped in front of her house she said, "I'd better go in through the back. My parents work long, hard hours and they need their rest. You can meet them after the prom," then kissed him lightly on the cheek and got out walking up the drive towards a small Toyota that was set just beyond the side view of the house.

Looking at the house, all the lights were off. After waiting a few minutes to make sure she got in safely, he noticed that the lights remained off but decided she was safely in and pulled away from the curb heading home.

When Randy drove into the garage, he didn't fail to notice that the lights in the living room and kitchen were still on. Thinking back, he remembered that at least one of his parents stayed awake until all the children were in the house safely and in their beds before going to bed themselves; even when he worked long into the night, someone was always up and awake.

He wondered why Catlin's parents didn't do the same, especially with her being the only child. Surely, they must love her as much as his parents loved him. Still, he wondered.

When he opened the back door to the kitchen, his mother and father were sitting at the kitchen table drinking cold coffee and eating pieces of the cake she had laid out when he and Catlin were leaving for the beach.

"Hi, there," Betty said as he came in the door carrying both the gym bag and the igloo. "I can see by the tan on your face that you got plenty of sun, but did you get any rest?"

Putting both items down and closing the door Randy said, "Yeah, I got rested. We both did, but we also had so much fun, I'm not so sure I got rested."

"It's not how much sleep the body gets that's called rest, but the changing of one's surroundings and breaking of daily habits by having a different enjoyment that actually causes the body to become rested." his father explained.

Pulling up a chair at the table, Randy poured himself a glass of milk. It seemed to him that he was expected because there was an empty glass, a fork, and a plate sitting on the table as though his parents had been waiting for him.

"You didn't have to wait up for me," he told them.

"Actually, we weren't," his father said. "Your mother and I were just talking, and I guess the time just flew by. But, we weren't waiting for you. Since we are up, and by the look on your face, it looks like you need someone to talk to anyway," Randy Carr Senior told his son.

"It's been a confusing, fun-filled, and emotional day, and I haven't had time to sort through everything yet," Randy said sheepishly.

"From that look on your face, I'd say I've got a pretty good idea about the emotional confusion," Betty stated.

Randy Senior was now looking at his son in a confused manner then said to both of them, "Other than seeing an unfinished tan, you look good."

Betty laughed a little and said to her failing husband, "The boy has been bitten by a bug."

Randy's sudden realization that there must be a welt somewhere he failed to notice started looking at his arms and running his hands over his face and neck before he looked back at his laughing mother.

65

Placing a gentle hand over her son's hand, she stopped laughing and explained. "Not that kind of bug, Randy. It's called LOVE, as in the 'love bug'."

His father took another long look at his son, then looked deep into the boy's eyes. He had been bitten only once in his lifetime, that by his wife of nineteen years and he never felt the prick of the bite as it penetrated his heart because they were both ten years old. Theirs was a love that had grown out of childhood and only matured over the next thirty plus years. But tonight, he looked upon his only son with a new sense of awe and smiled saying, "Once bitten is enough for any man."

And it was true; the man now sitting across from him was no longer the boy of yesterday.

"This Catlin must be something if she has bitten you this hard," he told his son. "I'm looking forward to meeting her and her family soon."

"Dad, she knows full well about my long work hours, plus the extra time I plan on putting in college during the summer," Randy informed him.

"And?" Betty inquired. "What did you expect her to say?"

"Honestly, Mom, I don't know. But I've got a gut feeling she's gonna stick around," Randy said.

"She knows you've got a good future," his father told him. "Perhaps she feels that you are worth waiting for. But remember Randy, she hardly knows you yet."

"I'll grant you that one," his mother agreed. "I like her, too. You are both young and your relationship is also new. Tomorrow, things could be different; but after seeing how she looks at you, I don't expect her feelings to falter much, if any," she told her son.

They sat and talked for another hour then headed for bed. Six a.m. came all too early in the Carr house.

The prom was now three days away. Randy had a lot on his mind as he headed out of the driveway to take Tammy to school because she missed the bus.

"You look like you got sun burned, you're bright red," Tammy told him. "Are you gonna see Catlin today?"

"Yeah, this morning, anyway. I'll get out of school at one and head for a long night doing research on a lawsuit. We've got to get the defense ready by next Tuesday," he told her.

As they pulled into the school, there was a light drizzle and Tammy said prior to getting out, "Tell Catlin hi for me," then disappeared through a set of doors.

Betty had given Randy a handwritten note for why he hadn't gone to school the day before. It was the first day he'd missed since the fifth

67

grade.

Leaving Edgewood Middle School, Randy pulled out on Garden Drive and was nearly hit broadside. He didn't see the other car coming from his side. Thankfully, the other driver was driving defensively.

After the near collision, Randy's heart was ready to explode. He realized that he had been thinking about Catlin and how much she was changing his life. He didn't realize that growing up was going to be so hard.

Once he had gathered himself, he checked both directions, and then pulled back on Garden heading the two blocks to Edgewood. There he turned left and went the six blocks to where Edgewood crossed Ellington where Micky D's was located. Going through the drive thru, he ordered two cherry Danishes, two OJ's, and two hot chocolates to help take the chill of the drizzle out of his and Catlin's bones.

When he approached Roosevelt, he looked to where the bus stop was, and nearly panicked when he didn't see Catlin.

On both sides of Edgewood there were stores for about four blocks. The last place he looked was towards the Edgewood Theater, the bus stop was directly across from there. Randy never looked again to his left.

Not seeing Catlin caused his heart to almost stop. It was then that

Randy Carr knew he was hooked.

Thinking he'd drive over to her house and pick her up, he needed to make a u-turn. Looking both directions, he nearly pulled out heading back towards her house when there was a sudden loud knock on the window on the passenger side of the car.

He almost peed on himself, he wasn't expecting it. When he jerked his head around, he saw a very wet face peering at him through the side window. It was a face he wasn't sure he knew through the rain drops that coated the window.

"Hey, open the door," the voice said.

Popping the auto locks on his door, the passenger door opened and a drowned rat in a blue dress flopped into the seat.

Randy still didn't recognize his guest until she parted her wet brown hair and smiled at him. "Good morning," Catlin said.

"My God, I didn't recognize you. You're drowned. Don't you have a rain coat or at least an umbrella?" Randy asked. "Hey!" he finally calmed down, "I didn't mean to snap at you, but I almost got hit broad-side a few minutes ago, and I didn't see you at the bus stop. My nerves are a little frazzled," he apologized.

Before he could pull out into the oncoming traffic, and before she put on her seat belt, she, without uttering a word, planted a very wet and warm kiss on his lips, shutting him up for a few still confused moments.

"You can't go to school like that. We'll be late, but I'll drive you home so you can dry off and change. I could have picked you up at home," he suggested.

"I can't go home right now. There's something going on and I'd rather not go back until later," she told him. "Besides, I won't melt you know. I've been wet before," she said laughingly.

"Are you in trouble because of yesterday?" Randy asked.

"No, of course not. I told you my parents are very understanding and only wanted to know if I had fun and whether or not you relaxed and got some rest," Catlin insisted.

"Then why can't you go home at least long enough to dry off and change?" he questioned her.

"I can't because my parents have a special guest and there was a death. I wouldn't fit in right now."

"Well, I can't take you to school like that; Mom would have me skinned," he told her.

"Come on, we'll go back to my house, I'll call school and tell them we're gonna be late. I've already got an excuse for yesterday, so I'm sure I can swing things. Besides, Mom's out for the day and I know she won't mind," Randy said convincingly.

"Are you sure?" she asked.

"Yeah, we'll be okay. I can dry your dress and you can wrap up in my bathrobe until your dress is ready," he assured her, then turned the car towards home.

Knowing it was the right thing to do, he didn't hesitate, and within ten minutes they were pulling into the driveway.

Since his parents were not home, he pushed a button on his key ring and the garage door opened automatically and he pulled into the dry garage, closing the door once inside. Getting out, he unlocked the door to the kitchen and they went in.

As it turned out, Betty, before leaving the house, had transferred the beach towels into the dryer before leaving the house for the day, and the machine had just shut off minutes ago.

Feeling the warmth of the dryer as they walked by it, Randy opened the door and pulled out one hot and dry towel and handed it to Catlin to dry off with as he led her up to his room to change into his robe so he could put her dress in the dryer.

Saying it shouldn't take too long, perhaps half an hour at most and we won't miss more than one class.

71

"I'll call the school after I put your dress in the dryer to let them know we'll be a little late," he finished as she slipped out of her dress and bra and panties and into his robe.

Catlin followed him back out the door and asked, "Do you think your mother would mind me using her hairbrush to do my hair? If I don't do it now, it'll get all tangled."

"I don't think so. You go ahead. I'll meet you in the kitchen when you're ready," he told her.

After folding the towels and the other things Betty had in the dryer, Randy put the items in with a Bounty Softener and took the towels and other things to the upstairs linen closet and put them away.

Not seeing Catlin in passing, he stuck his head in his parent's room to find Catlin sitting in front of the mirror his mother used gently brushing her long brown hair.

Coming up behind her, he said "Here, give me that for a minute." He then did as he had watched his father do so many times to his mother and began to   brush long strokes of Catlin's fine silky hair when he whispered, "The rain water must have made it softer." He didn't remember hitting any snags.

They sat there quietly brushing for what seemed a lifetime when Catlin put her hand over his stopping him. "I think my dress must be dry by now," she said as she turned to face him still holding his hand. The front of his robe opened partly revealing her bare breast.

He knew they didn't have time, but before he could say anything, she slipped out of his arms and headed for the door.

Since his room was between her and the stairs, he at first thought she intended to go to his room until he saw that she was indeed going downstairs.

Catching up to her, he followed her down and through the living room to the kitchen, then to the garage where the washer and dryer were.

Seeing the machine had stopped, she opened the door taking out her dress and underclothes and turned to Randy and asked, "Did you remember to call the General?"

"No, I completely forgot. It's too late now. We'll have to go to the office during the day between classes and explain," he told her.

"Randy," Catlin said, "I'm sure this kind of thing happens all the time. I mean about some student getting caught in a downpour and having to go back home to change," then turned towards the living room and the stairs saying, "I won't be but a couple of minutes."

Watching her go, he wanted to go with her, but knowing he had to work later and that it might be another all-nighter, and at the very least, a very long afternoon, he let her go.

73

"Hey, I forgot the hot chocolate," he thought to himself and went to the car to retrieve both cups and lifting the lids, popped them into the microwave, setting the timer for twenty seconds, then went to the cupboard and found some miniature marshmallows.

Catlin walked in fully dressed and ready to go just as the microwave beeped twice, indicating the chocolate was ready.

Not knowing what the double beeping sound was, she asked, "Ready?"

"Almost," he answered. "I put some hot chocolate in the microwave, it just beeped. I hope you like marshmallows in it."

"I'm a girl. Of course I like marshmallows. What's a microwave?" she asked innocently.

One of the things Randy had learned about Catlin was that not only was she old fashioned, she really didn't know about modern electronics. If he asked the wrong question, he might regret saying the wrong thing.

"Perhaps," he thought to himself, *"her family is afraid of the new electronic generation."* He had heard of many kids at Lee whose family couldn't afford computers or cell-phones, and had trouble dealing and adjusting with them while at school.

"Back to Dad's Rule of Thumb," he figured...

"It's an electronic oven that uses radiation instead of conventional heat, not unlike a stove. Just be careful, the cups might be very hot," he explained.

Watching her, he saw her trying to pull the door open, then said, "You have to pull the handle towards your left," then it popped open and she carried the cups very carefully setting them on the counter next to the marshmallows.

"I'm not sure what makes them work," he told her honestly.

After putting a handful of marshmallows in both cups, they locked up and headed out for school.

One hour twenty minutes late, they both walked into the school and after a brief kiss, they parted ways at a crosswalk glancing back after her he couldn't believe his eyes. She was gone in the blink of an eye. *"She must be in one of the first two rooms,"* he thought, but because he was already five minutes late for his computer class, he didn't take the time to look into either of the two rooms.

It seemed that the day flew by. He remembered to stop by the office and give his written excuse to the student secretary and explained that his girlfriend had gotten drenched and he took her home to change.

"We had over sixty kids get caught in it," she told him, then wrote down both of their names and he left.

At 12:40, he was let out of his History class and headed for the parking lot, but peered into both rooms that he thought Catlin might have gone in, but neither had classes in them. He left scratching his head about how one person could so suddenly disappear before his very eyes.

When he got to the office, he found Wendy, Frances, and John just getting out of their cars and he held up two large bags of Dunkin Donuts, smiling.

"How's the new girlfriend?" Wendy asked.

"Hey," John said. "Who's got a new girlfriend?"

"Not me," Frances told them. "I can't afford one."

They all laughed and each looked at Wendy, and did a second look at Randy, whose face was still beet red from the day before.

"Looks like Randy's got a new 'bud,'" Frances exclaimed, "and it looks like the 'bud' bug has really taken a bite out of him," as they all laughed.

"Actually," Randy responded coolly, "My mother thinks she's in for a long hard ride, but she also told dad that she likes her and expects she has the staying power to see me through college."

"You'll meet her at the prom, and you'll see why I think she's more than just a 'Bud'," then they all went in and got to work.

At their law office, an intern either receives no pay but receives a full scholarship at the firm's favorite college, or receives 10% of their salary plus a full scholarship or a partial one depending their final grades during their first few years in college.

Here, things were different because each of this firm's interns was more than committed to a law degree. Each was totally committed to the way this firm handled their business.

Every intern hence not only sat in on the actions with the firm's clientele, they actually ran the investigations, filed suits, plead cases, and interviewed new clientele, building a solid rapport with the new clients and learning from the Seniors as they grew.

While no action was taken without a Senior's approval, the interns ran the office, and they were well paid by the Seniors for their services.

Wendy, and later Randy during their first year at the firm, helped to bring in over a dozen new clients. Most were young people forming new businesses that later would, through careful molding by the firm's Seniors, build bridges between other clientele who over time help support, and even on occasion, outright join one business to another or add strength to one another.

This gave the law firm stronger, more stable clientele and less trouble with unstable, new inexperienced clients.

The kids added the building blocks, the Seniors the solid foundation. A suit brought against one was likened to a suit against the firm itself and thankfully, those were few.

The case the interns were working on now was a defense for a client who supplied battery packs to a new cell phone. The Plaintiff charged the firm with knowingly purchasing, using, and supplying to the public a product that caused a fire.

The fire itself was minor. The cause was an overcharged battery that got hot enough to ignite the Plaintiff's suit jacket.

In and of itself, that seemed minor. Simply buy the man a new suit. But this man was not just any Joe Blow" off the street, he was OSHA, and the only suit he wanted had way too many zeros in the price and the only suit he would settle for was a big check.

It was the interns' job to find and build a strong defense against a man who had a governmental department supporting his claim. It was to be an uphill battle each step of the way.

That night came a breakthrough. Randy and Frances found their defense and got it pulled up on the computer. It seemed that a law firm in Seattle had a similar case where it went all the way to the highest court. Each step was denied by all the courts and the Plaintiff just kept throwing good money after bad. The only ones who won were the lawyers.

The item, being a TV battery pack in this case, had to have two basic elements to be held accountable for injuries, but in this case, there were none. First a governmental test must have been done showing manufacturer default.

The governmental agency in any case rarely gets involved until there are several cases and complaints. In the case at bar, it was the only such case.

Next, the complainant must show a case history of the like on almost any item it made to show cause for public concern.

Again, in the case at bar, the manufacturer had a sterling record going back nearly fifty years, and its own open records were verified by several safety groups around the world.

In this case, there was a third element which was common in all cases won. That being that the client had to be directly involved in both the manufacturing of said product and in its ongoing testing. Of which this client was only a retail outlet and couldn't be held liable for any amount other than the price of the product. He was not even liable for the cost of the man's suit. End of Story!

It was now 10:45 P.M.; their bosses were happy, the client had been contacted and he was happy. The Plaintiff would be held responsible for all attorney fees, and the billing hours would be extremely high. All in all, it was a wonderful night for everyone! When the most senior

79

partner read the case, he finished with a large bonus for each of his research staff and gave them the rest of the week off.

When Randy drove into his driveway at home, he was floating on cloud nine. He noticed the lights were on in the back of house and went in the back door to find his mother.

"I hope you weren't waiting for me," he told her.

"No, no, I just got involved in a novel and couldn't put it down. Then she noticed the time and asked, "Did your boss finally find his heart or did you quit?" Betty teased him.

Randy took out the folded bonus check his boss had given him and laid it on the table before his mother.

"WOW! What did you do to rob him of all this?" she asked.

"Frances and I found the key that will save our client his bread and butter and our firm possibly millions of dollars in fines and court costs; that's all," Randy said stretching as though bored over the small matter.

"Randy!" Betty told her son. "There's enough money right here to put a hefty deposit on a house or cover your expenses in college for the next three or four years without you needing to work yourself to death."

Now, grinning at his mother, he said "So I can spend a lot more time with Catlin."

"Hmm," she said, "now I see why you're so high and happy."

"Yup!" he said and headed for the stairs, a shower, and a great night of dreaming. "Nite, Mom," was all he said as he turned from her.

Getting up from the table, Betty Carr turned out the kitchen lights and followed her son up the stairs to her sleeping husband.

The morning before the prom, Randy picked up Catlin and headed for school. They spent the morning's ride talking about the prom, when Catlin asked him some questions.

"Randy, you told me that you love me, and I believe you, but if spending eternity with me meant giving up your dream of law school, would you?"

Randy, thinking his love for her was being tested, gave much thought to how he should answer and he knew his answer would have to be honest if he truly loved this girl. "I could simply say yes, or no, but that wouldn't be the type of answer you'd want to hear. Is an answer today, right this minute, so important that I would have to choose one over the other here and now? You already know I'd choose you over anything, but I'd also have to justify my decisions to myself, and for that I'd have to have time to think things through," he explained.

81

He began to think out loud with her as his conscience and guide saying "You know how important the money would be in our future, buying a home and all the things that are needed to make it a comfortable home for you and our children later on."

"Randy, if I were to tell you that no matter what you might earn, no matter where we spend our eternity, money would never enter into the love we share now, nor would it in an eternity, that we might never have children, could you love me no matter what, the future might or might not hold for us? Could you still love me and would you still want to spend an eternity with me at your side?"

"Wow," he said. "'That's a lot to consider. Not to change the subject, but can I drive you home after school?" They were only a block from the General at that moment. "Perhaps I can answer some of your questions then."

Reaching over, she kissed him on the cheek and said softly, and in earnest, "Yes, you can take me home later and perhaps you will find the answers you seek in your heart by then."

The school administration didn't know which students didn't have to work, so they were all turned out as usual, and Randy had completely forgot to tell Catlin that he was getting out early. He had been so befuddled that he completely forgot to tell her, so when he got to the car he wasn't all that surprised not to find her there waiting for him.

He needed time to think things through and to consider all that Catlin had placed before him. Since it would be two hours before school let out for the day, he decided to leave the car and take a walk where he could do some heavy thinking.

Leaving the parking lot, Randy's mind was totally on Catlin and her questions. He was sure that he loved her and for all the right reasons.

As he walked down one sidewalk, he began fingering his high school ring, turning it one way, then the other unconsciously. He had been walking for about forty-five minutes when he found himself standing before a Baptist Church. Without thought or hesitation, he walked over the walkway and towards the front doors. *"I don't remember ever seeing a church around here,"* he thought to himself as he pulled open the door leading into the chapel.

He hadn't gone very far into the building when he found himself seated on one of the back row benches. There seemed to be some sort of music being piped in and it soothed his restless spirit.

"I know you don't know me, Lord, but I need someone special to talk to. I don't know how I got here, but will you hear me out and give me some idea as to what I should say? Catlin is the woman I love and want very much to spend my eternity with. But I don't understand her love. I don't really understand love at all," he said quietly.

It was then that a voice came to him saying, "Son, love is not something to be understood. Just accepted and cherished, shared and nourished by those who seek and find it."

Startled, Randy almost jumped until he spied a man sitting next to him, whom he hadn't noticed before.

"I'm sorry," Randy said quietly, "I didn't see you and didn't mean to intrude."

"You not intruding, Son. Perhaps I can help you find some answers. My name is Hank Snowden. This is my church. Would you like something to drink? I've got a couple of cokes in my office frig," Pastor Snowden offered.

"Thank you, Pastor, but I'm not even a member of your church," Randy explained.

"That's alright son, most people who come in here aren't, but it doesn't mean you can't enjoy a coke and a talk with someone," he suggested, leading Randy towards a side door he hadn't noticed when he first came in.

"My name is Randy Carr, I'm a senior at the General," he began. "My girlfriend is Catlin Hyde, who's a junior; we met two weeks ago."

Randy was very open and extremely honest and frank with his host, then spent the next hour explaining all that had taken place excluding nothing, which did not shock or surprise the pastor.

When Randy had finished telling all to the friendly-faced man, he listened to some sound advice finished with this thought, "Son, I've heard many an interesting and enlightened story over the years, and the best I can offer is for you to sleep on it, but not dwell on it. When it comes time for you to give your answers, let your heart speak for you. You have repeatedly stated your love for Catlin, and I, like you, believe that love is both honest and true. In your own way, you must learn to trust in that love, both in what you bring to this relationship, and what Catlin will bring. Remember too, she is giving her all to you; can you give her less? And if you do, would it be fair to either of you?"

Then, they prayed the 23rd Psalms and Pastor Snowden walked him to the door.

The sun was bright and warm on his face as Randy walked with a lightened step to the corner and got his bearings. He was only three blocks from school and would be back just as the last class was letting out. He only hoped Catlin would wait for him.

Rounding the corner, he noticed that most of the parking lot was already empty and that there were very few kids milling about. He knew he had been gone a long time, but he hadn't looked at his watch. This was a day he needed time to think.

Was he ready to make such a final commitment? He gave Pastor

Snowden's words much thought, especially his suggestion to sleep on it for a night. "You can give your answer tomorrow, and you'll have felt better for having waited a day," he told the young man.

Peering at the watch he wore on his left wrist, he noticed that the time had stopped. Had he not looked at his watch all day? It read 7:55. When was the last time he had looked at it? Thinking back, he couldn't remember.

Entering the parking lot from the street, Randy was almost overwhelmed to see Catlin did indeed wait for him, and didn't seem at all too surprised to see him coming from the street rather than the school building.

"You waited!" Randy said.

"Of course I waited. You don't know how long I've waited for you," she offered.

"I hope it wasn't too long. I guess I got lost in time and thought," he concluded.

Smiling as she kissed him, she said, "Randy, I waited a lifetime for you to find me. I can wait a little longer," as he popped the electronic locks on the doors.

Randy opened the door on her side and let her slip into the hot seat. She didn't say a word about how hot it was.

Leaving the door open on her side, Randy told her, "leave it open until I get mine open. The breeze will blow the hot air out while I put the top down."

"Okay," she said as he walked around the car and opened his door.

Randy decided that both he and Catlin liked having the top down on his Mustang and wondered why all car companies didn't make the four door family car with detachable tops. Then he remembered that back in the late fifties and the early sixties that Ford had made only one car, the Lincoln Continental convertible, with four doors. Anyway, as he popped the locks on his side of the roof, he still thought a lot of families would enjoy having the breeze and the warmth of a top down convertible on a family sedan.

"Ready?" Randy asked. "I'm glad I don't have to work tonight." Then thought to ask, "Do you have plans for dinner?" remembering that her parents worked late into the night, and that she might enjoy eating dinner with him and his family.

"I normally just fix something, do my homework and go to bed early, why?" she asked.

"You could eat dinner with us. We've plenty of food and room. Mom and Dad would love to have you over, that is," he said "if your parents wouldn't mind. Since we still have half a day of classes tomorrow, I can drive you home later," he suggested.

"Mom and Dad won't be home until after 10, so as long as I'm in before then, there shouldn't be any problems," she answered. "Are you sure your folks wouldn't mind?"

"Heck no," Randy answered honestly, then reached in the glove box and pulled out his cell phone and said, "Here, I'll call her."

Catlin, having never used a cell phone, even though she had seen many people talking on them during the last few weeks, said, "You live in a day of marvels: having cell phones, computers, color televisions and all the other gadgets. It must be nice."

Not really paying all that close attention to the exact wording Catlin had used because he was waiting for his mother to pick up, just kind of said, "Yeah, sometimes it's great.

"Hi, Mom." Randy said. "Can Catlin have dinner with us? Her parents are working late again, and I thought she might enjoy some company," he suggested.

"That's fine, we're having spaghetti, and if you would, could y'all stop by the Winn Dixie and pick up some French bread?" Betty asked.

"Okay, mom. Thanks. Love ya. We'll be there in about an hour," Randy told her, then hung up and put the phone in his shirt pocket saying, "Mom wants us to stop by the store on our way home. Do you need to pick up anything from home?" he asked thoughtfully.

"No. I don't need anything," she replied.

"I've given a lot of thought to your questions," Randy told her as they pulled out of the parking lot. "If you don't mind, someone once told me that if I could, I should sleep on things for at least one night before making such important decisions and or choices."

"No. Tomorrow is good enough. I can wait one more day. That is if you are sure you even want to answer my questions," she told him.

Lee Charles Daniels

Chapter 4

Gone as time fell to
The rustle of leaves
Strengthened by the stones

Stopping at the Winn Dixie, Randy went first to the bread aisle to check the prices, then to the bakery. Catlin was fascinated by all the fresh scents of the baked goods. "They smell delicious," she exclaimed.

"I'm glad I don't work in a store like this," Randy said. "I'm afraid I'd gain another hundred pounds with just the smell. And God help me if I ever started sampling everything, I'd really put the pounds on. Working with my brain, I burn more calories than any physical exercise could burn off of me, but I think working in a place like this during the summer would be a true challenge to that theory," he concluded as he picked out a loaf he thought would be enough for the entire family.

Going to the register to pay, he opened his wallet, taking out five dollars, when Catlin laughed saying, "0h, so you do still use real money once in awhile."

"Yeah," he said, then explained, "I usually use my debit card, but with the high cost of using it on small items, it just makes sense to use cash on purchases under five dollars."

Getting back in the car and as they were starting to back out of the space, a jet black Chevy Camaro screeched to a halt less than two inches from Catlin's side door. Randy's heart almost stopped because he saw the car coming at a high rate of speed and could do nothing to stop the events had he known what to do.

By the time the car came to a full stop, Randy could not see any of the front end on the Camaro nor could he see the first three quarters of the car's hood.

Catlin, thankfully never saw or knew how close she came to being broadsided. Randy thinking to himself thought, "*Damn, at the rate of speed that car was coming, it would have crushed the entire side of the car, possibly killing Catlin,*" without him being able to lift a hand to stop it.

He took a deep breath and let it out slowly, when Catlin noticed his strange behavior and asked, "Are you alright?"

Still looking past her caused her to turn to see what he was looking at, then   saw that the driver of the other car was also as pale looking as Randy. It was then she realized what had taken place and exclaimed, "Randy, I'm alright. It's alright. He didn't hit us."

Seeing that he had made her more unsettled, Randy composed himself remembering that this was twice in under a week that he was nearly broadsided and vowed to become a better defensive driver in the

92

future.

All of this had taken place within a mere two or three second time span, then he said a small prayer of thanks and pulled away from the parking lot and into the main stream of the evening travelers all working their way home to their families and dinner. "Is this how my life will be from here on?" he asked himself.

Looking at Catlin sitting at his side, he decided there and then that this was indeed what he wanted in his life as he reached over taking her hand in his, tenderly but firmly.

"After seeing how close I just came to losing you back there, I'm thankful you weren't hurt," he started and added, "I'm also sure about my love for you, whatever you ask of me, I'll do so I can love you, protect you, to do whatever it might take to always have you at my side forever."

Not saying a word, Catlin just smiled a knowing and assuring smile at him.

It took another ten minutes to reach Randy's house. Once there, Catlin carried the loaf of bread as they entered the back door going into the kitchen.

There Betty, Tamara, and Mary were busy putting bowls of salad together, or stirring the sauce for the spaghetti as the long noodles simmered.

Betty, seeing her new favorite visitor, stopped long enough to give Catlin a hug and peck on the cheek as she introduced her to another of her daughters when Catlin asked, "What can I do?"

Before Betty could answer, Mary took Catlin by the hand and said, "Come on, you can help me set the table," and headed to the cabinet to retrieve plates and saucers. Pointing to their silverware drawer, she said "We need settings for five. The twins use their own."

"By the way," Betty said to Randy, "The twins are in the dayroom watching TV. While we finish up in here, why don't you take them upstairs and get them washed up before your father gets home."

Then turning to Catlin, Betty said "After y'all finish setting the table, you can go up to my room and freshen yourself before dinner. You already know where everything is."

"Thank you, that'll be fine." Then, the two girls turned to the dining room.

Leaving the kitchen, Randy followed the girls into the dining room where he said, "Hey, Baby," and bent over to kiss his sister on the cheek.

When Catlin saw that she smiled and walked around the large table and up to him, planting a very warm kiss upon his lips.

"Thank you," Catlin told him.

"You're welcome, but for what?" he asked.

"For you and for all of this," she opened her arms to take everything in around her.

Mary, seeing Catlin's love for her brother said, "It's not all friends and flowers, but we do have good times, too." Then asked, "Do you have a large family?"

"No, just my mother and father," Catlin answered. "But being here now, I feel more at home than anywhere I've ever been."

Betty, overhearing the conversation coming in the room says, "You are as much a part of this family as you want to be and will always be a welcome sight."

"I hope you'll always feel this way," Catlin told her.

"Oh, I'm sure we'll have our days, but it's all part of being a family. The rough days are as important to the strength of a family as are the good days," Betty assured her.

"Dinner will be ready in about fifteen minutes," she announced.

"Randy, you'd better get the twins ready before your father gets home."

"Okay, Mom. I'm on my way," then headed for the dayroom, or what is commonly called the family room, where the twins were enjoying themselves playing with each other.

"Hey guys, it's time to get cleaned up for dinner," he told them giving each a big bear hug and a kiss.

"I have a surprise for you," Randy told them.

"Really?" Trisha asked.

"What surprise, Randy?" Tarsha asked.

"We have a new friend who's gonna eat dinner with us. Her name is Catlin, and she goes to school with me," Randy told them as they headed up the stairs.

"Is she pretty?" Tarsha asked.

"Is she your girlfriend, Randy?" Trisha asked.

"Yes to both questions," Randy answered honestly.

"I have a boyfriend," Mary confided in Catlin, holding her voice down so her mother couldn't hear. "He's not old   enough to drive a car yet, but we go to school together and talk a lot," she told her new friend.

"I won't tell," Catlin promised as they finished setting the table.

"Hello, the house" came a baritone voice from the living room. Betty and the girls came out of the kitchen, each carrying a platter of food as Randy Senior noticed the extra plate and chair set at the table before he ever saw Catlin.

Stepping into view, Randy Carr stepped into his past. A past he had long forgotten.

Twenty-five years before, he had known a girl, one he had known only from afar. This night, he was facing the same girl only it couldn't be the same girl. "*Perhaps her daughter, only that couldn't be either*," he thought. The girl he had dreamed about as a young man had died. "*But my God,*" he thought.

"Do I know you?" Randy Carr Senior asked dumbfounded.

"Perhaps in another day you did," Catlin teased him.

Then Betty spoke to Randy Carr Senior, "This is Catlin Hyde, Randy's date for the prom tomorrow."

Automatically putting out his right hand, Randy shook the girl's hand as Randy and the twins came running into the room. Each was eager to meet Randy's girlfriend, but first greeted their father with a big hug and kiss.

Looking at the identical twins, Catlin squatted down and said, "You must be Trisha and Tarsha," giving each of the youngsters a big hug.

97

"You're as pretty as Tamara said," Trisha exclaimed.

"Randy, can she sit next to me?" they both asked hopefully.

"She'll sit next to Randy, where she belongs," Mary told them.

"Ah," they said as they headed for their places at the table.

"I'll be right down," Randy Senior told them as he kissed them and headed for the stairs to wash up.

Tamara said to Catlin, "You sit here, next to Randy. That's where you belong."

"Alright, you guys settle down," Betty told her gaggle of youngsters.

When Randy's father joined them and everyone had settled in, Betty told her guest, "Every meal we share at the table together, we take a moment to remember our troops who are fighting overseas."

No one spoke for about a minute, then Tamara said, "I'm hungry."

Randy Senior laughed and said, "Okay, but you know the rules, our guest gets her's first, then he who brought her into the house."

"I know, Daddy," Trisha said as she turned towards Catlin and said, "You're beautiful," turning towards her father she said, "Isn't she, daddy?"

"Yes, she is very pretty," he readily agreed.

During dinner there was much talk about the next day's events. Tamara said, "I hope next year I can go to the prom, I've already picked out the dress I want to wear."

"You mean that blue and pink one we saw at the mall last week?" Mary asked. "The colors suit your red hair perfectly."

"Beautiful, isn't it?" Tamara said.

"I think it will be even more beautiful when it is on you." Betty told her eldest daughter.

After dinner, the table having been cleared, Randy announced "I've got to pick up my tux, and we need to go before they close."

Everybody said their goodbyes and he and Catlin left.

In the car, Catlin said, "Randy, I really love your family. Being an only child can be extremely lonesome at times."

"You're not alone anymore," Randy assured her as she squeezed his hand.

"Right now," Catlin told him, "I feel more alive than I've ever felt."

"We've got a lot more living ahead of us, and my family will always be there for us," Randy told her.

"Randy, we don't always know what our tomorrows might hold for us. It could all end in the blink of an eye today," she told him. "Right now is all we've got. Your family is more alive than I'm used to, and I like every one of them."

"There are days when I wish they weren't so lively, but it's always fun, Catlin." Randy went on, "Everyone in my family really likes you. Dad even said that he felt he'd known you even before he met my mother. Mom said if he had met you before her, he'd still be with you today. But that's just talk."

"Your father is a handsome man, but he is just a little too old for me," she teased. "Besides, I'm happy being with you," she told him honestly.

"I hope you'll still think that after an eternity," Randy said without realizing the exact words he had spoken.

Smiling to herself, she put on the tape of Elvis singing "The Chapel of Love" and they both happily sang along.

"Do you want to go with me to pick up my tux?" Randy asked.

"No. I think not. I want to be as surprised as you'll be when we see each other for the first time before the dance tomorrow," she told him.

Then the Beach Boys began singing "California Girls" and they continued on towards Catlin's house.

While it was still early in the evening, Catlin said before they turned onto Darcey Street, "Let me off here. I want to see a friend before I go home."

Complying, Randy made the turn and pulled over to the curb. Catlin undid her seatbelt and kissed Randy before saying, "Thank you, Randy. I really enjoyed myself tonight and I love you and your family. I'm really looking forward to tomorrow." Then kissed him again and said, "I love you more then you know, Randy Carr." Then she opened the door and stepped out and away from the car before Randy could say another word.

After picking up his tux, Randy returned home where he was met by his mother.

"Why are you home so early?" she asked.

"Actually," he stated "I think Catlin had things to do to get ready for tomorrow." Then he yawned and said, "I've got my things ready and we get out of school at noon. After school, I'm supposed to pick Catlin up at five so we can have an early dinner before the prom. I've made reservations at Rudy's for 5:30. The dance starts about 7:30, but I figured we'd get there about 8. That should leave us plenty of time to enjoy ourselves," he concluded.

"Don't forget to stop by here after dinner so I can get some pictures and y'all can pick up your buttons and bows." Betty reminded her son.

101

"Now, why don't you turn in early, you look like you could use a little extra rest."

In agreement, Randy kissed his mother on the cheek and said, "Goodnight" as he headed for the stairs. "See you in the morning," he finished.

ℭ

Friday morning, Randy was up at 6am. He quickly showered and dressed. As he sat at the kitchen table enjoying a cold glass of Mott's Apple Juice, Randy Senior and his mother joined him.

"I'm glad y'all came down. I need to talk to you before I head for school," Randy told his parents.

"The coffee is ready," he offered.

"Thanks," Betty said as she poured her husband and herself a cup.

"I'm gonna guess," his father said, "that this has something to do with Catlin."

"Son," Betty told him as she handed Randy Senior his cup of hot coffee, "since that girl came into this house, I've felt an electricity that has charged every fiber in the air."

His father told him, "You know that on the night of my senior prom, I proposed to your mother."

Randy missed seeing his mother place a small square box on the table next to her cup of coffee.

"I'm gonna ask Catlin to marry me," Randy almost shouted at his parents.

Sliding the little box towards her son, Betty said "This belonged to your grandmother. She wanted me to pass it down to you when the time came."

Randy had never seen the small box before, nor had he ever paid any attention to what such a small box like it might hold.

Dumbfounded, he picked up the box as he watched his father take his mother's hand into his, then slowly opened the box.

Prior to turning in the night before, Randy had gone online to several local jewelers looking for just the right ring, but not finding any to his liking. Now, opening the box his mother placed in front of him, he viewed the most perfect ring. Looking up at his parents for the first time, Randy Carr Junior was speechless.

His mother got up and went around the table to where Randy sat and put her arms around him and kissed his cheek saying, "We knew this was what you wanted. We both did. Your Father and I think she's exceptional and we are happy for both of you."

"Son," his father asked, "Are you gonna wait until you graduate from college?"

Still speechless, Randy said thoughtfully, "I haven't had time to think that far ahead yet."

"Six years is a long time to wait," Betty reminded her son.

"I think if Catlin accepts, and after we discuss everything, I should let her decide how long we should wait. I'm thinking two years at least. It's going to be hard enough on both of us as she still has to graduate from high school," Randy explained.

"I'm not even sure whether Catlin might want to go to college later or not and then there's what she might want to major in and how long that might take," he told them.

"Have you given any thought to whether her parents might object or insist on you finishing college first?" his father asked.

"Dad, I haven't even met Catlin's parents. While their feelings are very important, I'm not marrying them nor do I intend to live with them," Randy said.

"Last week, Mr. Smith gave out bonuses. That, along with my savings, I want to put a large deposit on a small starter home for us to live in," Randy told them.

Neither his father nor mother was very surprised hearing his tentative plans. This was a topic they had discussed at least a thousand times over the last ten years since each child had inherited a large sum of money from their grandparent's estate.

Looking at his parents, he reminded them that "Catlin hasn't even said yes. She may not even want to think about getting married until she graduates from high school, or she might want to go to college for her degree before she would even consider marriage. I just know in my heart how much I love her. Spending an eternity with her would be like spending a single day in the spring. If she wants to wait, we'll wait; no matter how long. But, mom," Randy said honestly, "I haven't even talked to her yet."

"Son," Betty told him, "if I read Catlin right, and I think I do, she'll not only say yes but will be willing to get married tomorrow if you asked her to. There is no question of her love for you. As for finishing school, if her parents won't help, I think between us, we can manage if she wants," Betty assured her son.

The time was fast approaching 7 A.M. Thanking God for having such loving parents. Randy hugged and kissed both of them, "I've got to get ready if I'm gonna pick Catlin up at 7:55," and headed for the stairway.

Before leaving the house, Randy again hugged his parents. The time was now 7:20 when he climbed in his bright red Ford Mustang convertible. Two minutes later, the top down, he backed out of the driveway, glancing back at the only home he'd ever known.

Randy had a lot on his mind as he turned on Bellaire Boulevard heading towards Edgewood and McDonalds. Questions he had never before thought of were now filling his head; questions that never entered his train of thought like whether or not he was really ready to take such a bold step into the realm of adulthood. Rather, he thought more about finding a house they could afford. He knew his job and boss would make sure they had enough income to keep up any house payments without Catlin having to work.

He had planned, after dropping Catlin off at home so she could prepare for an early dinner, to stop by the law office to have a talk with Mr. Smith about setting up a secured job while he was in college. He didn't want to have any outside distractions by trying to hold a second job.

After pulling into the parking lot of Micky D's, Randy went inside. He had a taste for some sweet pastries to go along with hash browns and scrambled eggs, and he wanted to pick out just what he thought Catlin might enjoy, rather than having someone else pick something she might not enjoy. But then, what did he really know about her taste, likes and dislikes?

Before getting back in the car, he suddenly took notice of a floral shop next to Micky D's. He looked at his watch, knowing he had plenty of time, then decided to buy Catlin something special.

Getting back into the car, he placed his gift on her seat next to their breakfast. He was satisfied with how the day was progressing. Randy Carr was a happy young man and it showed as he pulled to the curb where Catlin waited for him.

"Good morning, beautiful," he offered as he reached over placing the breakfast and gift in the rear seat.

"And good morning to you too, kind sir," Catlin replied playfully, and apparently in the same good mood Randy was in.

"Another good sign from the heavens," Randy thought, then she kissed him and made everything even better.

Her kiss was sweet and warm; perhaps, he thought, even a little sensual. Her scent was fresh and he thought *"I could never tire of waking up to that scent."* It was not so much a turn-on as it was an awakening to his senses.

She wore a cream-colored full dress with shades of pink and mauve intertwined through its pleats. Her hair hung long about her shoulders with a cream ribbon from her forehead to just behind her ears.

"I hope you're hungry," he offered.

"I'm starved," she told him as he handed her a platter of hash browns, scrambled eggs and buttered toast. She had already seen the cup   of orange juice on the built-in cup holder in front of her. They voraciously devoured the greasy fast food.

"There's coffee in the back," he informed her and she turned to see two more cups and a single bright yellow rose sitting in a crystal vase that was just tall enough to keep it from falling out.

Catching her breath, Catlin picked it up; forgetting about all else, "Oh, Randy, it's the most beautiful rose I've ever seen," then smelled its fragrance deeply and sighed. "Randy," she said quietly, "no one has ever given me flowers before. This one single rose I'll take to my grave to hold forever." Then she reached over and kissed him saying, "I learn to love you more every day."

Randy reached over, taking her hand since the traffic on Roosevelt seemed light this morning and said, "I hope and plan on giving you a lot of beautiful flowers, especially if you're going to glow like this every time you get them," then squeezed her hand for just another moment before needing it to steer through more traffic.

"I'm gonna set this on my desk all day. I'll be the envy of all the girls," Catlin told him proudly.

Satisfied with himself, Randy pulled in the school parking lot where Catlin helped secure the roof latch on her side. "Thank you for the great breakfast and the rose."

"We get out of school at 11:45 for the day. You wanna ride home?" Randy was sure she'd say yes, but felt he still needed to respect her enough not to assume anything.

"I'd hoped you'd ask. I can meet you here after we're let out," she replied. Then kissed him on the lips and vanished from his sight.

She's good at that, he thought to himself again. He would have liked to walk her to her first class, but she was already out of sight before he could even get the first word out.

All during school that morning, Randy thought a lot about the decisions he had made and how those decisions would forever change his life. He also realized that he was still only eighteen years old and both he and Catlin had a whole lifetime ahead of them.

No matter what area of his future life he examined, he could not see any area where Catlin wasn't a part of it. When he tried to remove her from an area, he suddenly felt empty and lost as though a large portion of himself was missing. He knew she was that missing element which brought joy and completion to the very structure of every area he thought his life might lead. A future without Catlin would make life worthless and unbearable to him, like all young people in love thought from time to time.

"Is that all this is?? he asked himself. *"Just young love?"*

He didn't have an answer to that question, and didn't want to dwell on it.

During a twenty minute break between classes, Randy had gone to his locker to put some books away for the long weekend. Every class and teacher insisted that no student should have anything more on their mind other than the prom.

"Hey, there," Wendy said approaching her own locker, which was next to his, to put her books away too.

"Hey, good looking," Randy replied kissing her on the cheek as he held her books long enough to free up her hands as she opened her locker.

"Are you ready for the big night?" she asked.

"It's bigger than you think, but yes, I'm ready," Randy answered.

"Where's your girlfriend?" Wendy asked.

"Probably on the other end of the campus, or stuck in some class. Anyway, I'm gonna pick her up after school and take her home.

"Then again at five for an early dinner at Rudy's downtown before the dance. Mom wants us to stop by between dinner and the prom for pictures. You know how my mother is when she gets a camera in her hands. Besides, everyone at home likes Catlin a lot and she seems taken by them too. For that, I'm very grateful," Randy told her.

"Well, I hope to meet her later," Wendy said as she kissed Randy on the cheek before disappearing in another gaggle of students like she had been swallowed up.

After school let out, Randy headed for the parking lot. For once, he got there ahead of Catlin and popped the locks on the doors, then reached in and undid the latches to the top. Forty-five seconds later, the top was down.

The weather was about 78°, normal for mid-May; showers were a ten percent chance, but in Jacksonville, there is always that chance. The puffy clouds in the sky just kinda hung there, not seeming to move, or rather not very much.

The air was fresh and tranquil, and Randy Carr was at peace with himself and the world around him.

No sooner had he secured the top, Catlin walked up waving and wearing a broad smile that touched his heart.

"Hello," he offered.

Before she could reply, Wendy and her boyfriend Steve walked up from the other direction saying hello to Randy.

111

Catlin had just reached Randy and gave him a tender kiss. "Hello to y'all too," he answered her greeting.

"Finally," Wendy said aloud. "We get to meet the mysterious Catlin who has stolen our friend's heart," as she held her hand out to Catlin. "I'm Wendy Frisk, and this is my boyfriend Steve Larmon."

Before Randy could introduce Catlin, she spoke up saying, "Hello. I'm Catlin Hyde," then held out her hand to Wendy and added, "This is my boyfriend, Randy Carr," and they all laughed.

The two girls hugged and the young men shook hands.

"Randy has told me a lot about you," Catlin told Wendy. "I'm glad he has someone his own age to work with. Do the other kids go to Lee?"

"Well," Wendy answered, "there are only five of us interns. Randy and I go here, the rest go to either Terry Parker, or are already in their first year of college, but rest assured, we will all be at the prom tonight."

They talked for about another five minutes, then Randy and Catlin left. "I like her," Catlin told Randy as they pulled out of the parking lot.

"I'm glad, because I believe you'll be seeing a lot of her in the future as we do a lot of our work from either her house or from mine," he told her.

"Are you gonna need help getting ready for tonight?" Randy asked.

112

"Mom said she's available if you want to pick up your things and let her."

"My parents are going to be gone again, so yeah, I could use a little help if she is sure," Catlin told him.

"Hand me the phone out of the glove box," Randy instructed as he looked for a safe place to pull over.

Reaching in she took the cell phone and started to hand it to Randy when he said, "Push the button, then punch in the letters 'MOM' and you'll hear it ring."

Catlin had seen him use the phone several times, but had never talked on one herself. When it rang twice, Betty picked up saying, "Hi, Randy. Are y'all out of school already?"

"Hello, Betty, it's me," Catlin answered. "Yes, we're out for the weekend. Randy said you've offered to help me get ready for tonight, my parents are gone again, and I could use a little help if you really don't mind."

"Have Randy drop you by here on his way to the office, and we'll get you ready by the time he gets home," Betty instructed her

"Okay, and thank you," Catlin said sincerely, then hung up, putting the phone back in the glove box.

"You didn't tell me you had to work today," Catlin said to Randy.

"Oh, I'm not working. I've a meeting with Mr. Smith about getting a raise after graduation," he explained.

"Betty didn't say that. I just assumed you were needed," she said.

"No, we're off until after finals next month. Mr. Smith says we need to keep our grades up. It's one of the main reasons why I wanted to join their company over several others," he told her.

"I need to stop by the house and I'll need about an hour to get things ready. Can you pick me up then?" Catlin asked.

"I could wait, if you want," he offered.

"No. I think if you were to come in, we'd never make the dance," she told him.

"Hmm.." he said and agreed. "How about I pick you up in, say, an hour-and-a-half? I can have my meeting and then come back. I'm sure it won't last that long."

"That's okay. It'll give me time to clean up before we leave," Catlin said.

Dropping Catlin off at her house, Randy called his mother, then headed for the office.

The Law Offices of Smith and Greet were located on the 14th floor of the Prudential Building at the foot of the Main Street Bridge on the south side of the St. John's River and it took Randy about fifteen minutes to get there.

Luck would have it that Mr. Smith was just concluding a briefing as he came into the main lobby. "Great," Mr. Smith said with a warm smile for one of his favorite interns. Come on in," he instructed his young intern.

"Thank you, Mr. Smith, for seeing me on such short notice," he said following the Senior partner of the firm into his extra-large and spacious office on the southeast corner of the building facing east, giving a fantastic view of the famed Jacksonville Riverwalk.

Offering Randy a seat usually occupied by a client, Ronald B. Smith offered Randy a soda from the half wet bar set to one corner. Having been in this office many times, Randy was not intimidated by its lush gray carpeting, or the many trophies and paintings that lined the four walls. Getting himself a Pepsi from the cooler, Randy sat back down directly in front of his boss's desk.

"Now, Randy, what brings you here on such an important day?" Mr. Smith asked.

Starting his rehearsed spiel, Randy began. "Sir, I've been here almost eight months. I love working here. In three weeks, I start college. That is, in part, thanks to you and the generous scholarship program you set up for me. You'll see how much I appreciate that over the coming years," Randy began.

"Randy," Smith said, "Your grasp of the law is greater than any intern we've ever had since we established the firm. I'm sure you are going to continue being a leader in your field of law as you grow. It is an area of law we've wanted to develop, but lacked the right person to run it, so your keen interest in corporate law shows great promise. I've had the privilege on several occasions to talk to not only your family about this matter, but your coworkers about how much you share with them. Your promise of hard work in the future is not in doubt," he answered the young man seated in front of him.

"Mr. Smith, there is still one person you still haven't met. She is the main reason I asked for this meeting," Randy told him.

"Ah. The part that gives you your drive," Smith smiled at him knowingly.

"It is my intent," Randy said, "to use the last bonus as a down payment on a small starter home near the university, and while I think my pay will be enough to cover expenses, I want to be assured Catlin won't have to break her back working to cover the unexpected. I'm hoping my work and work habits warrant a raise. It doesn't have to be much, but enough to cover taxes, health care, and a good life insurance policy. With this extra, I won't have to worry about the possibility of taking an outside job down the road," Randy concluded.

"Hmm," the elder Mr. Smith commented and then sat studying the young man for several seconds before he spoke.

These few seconds might have unsettled most people asking for a raise, but the contented look on Randy's face showed his boss his full commitment to him and his firm.

"How soon are you planning to take the plunge?" Smith teased him.

"Tonight, after dinner and before the prom, I intend to ask her to marry me. I want to leave the date up to her and her family, but my mother thinks it will be soon; perhaps after my first year in college. But, I'd marry her tomorrow if she asked," Randy told him as he placed the small ring box on the desk between himself and Mr. Smith.

Picking up the proferred box, Mr. Smith opened it, remembering the day he sat across from his boss almost asking for the same consideration. "This is beautiful, son; certainly you couldn't afford this on your salary." Knowing the payments alone would be greater than his entire paycheck.

"No, sir. It was my grandmothers. She left it to me to put on the finger of Catlin, who she never had the chance to meet," Randy explained.

"This morning I spoke to mom and dad who seemed to already know my plans. Mom had this in her pocket for me. She and dad had already talked this over and approved of my intentions," he finished.

Handing the ring back to Randy, Mr. Smith smiled again and told him. "Randy, most interns don't deserve a raise until their second or third year in college. However, as I already said, you have on many occasions proven your worth and commitment to this firm. Put together a proposal of what you think you'll need and submit it to me next week. I think you'll find me most generous," he concluded by getting up and going around the desk as Randy too rose and, taking the young man's hand, he said, "Congratulations, Randy. I hope you'll bring your young lady around to meet us soon," as he escorted Randy from the office.

"That took less than twenty minutes," Randy thought as he pulled out of the parking lot. He also thought that he and Catlin had a lot to talk about after the prom.

Driving down College Street heading towards Roosevelt Boulevard Randy passed by John Gorry Junior High, where he spent two years. The building must have been built in the late thirties or early forties. He remembered thinking his seventh grade English teacher was a very pretty redhead and was single then. She's married now with half a dozen redheaded children.

He crossed over King Street which was an alternate to Roosevelt when there was a traffic jam. King wound through the southwest area of near downtown and had at one point been the area where only the most wealthiest of Jacksonville's citizens lived.

Every lot was at least a full acre; every building was at least three stories mixed with either wrought iron or red brick fences. No one would have thought to maintain their own yards, and hired the best landscapers, if for no other reason than to compete with their neighbors. The results were still evident even though the contest ended back in the late eighties when growth again pushed the elite towards Normandy Landing where only the richest of the elite migrated, leaving these beautiful homes to be turned into condos and wealthy apartments where Mr. Smith owned several lots he now leased to the high and mighty.

North and east of the Saint John's River were older houses built in the late forties after the war, or in the early fifties after the Korean war. These homes were called shoeboxes back then: small lots that were not much bigger than fifty-by-fifty or fifty-by-100-feet, and couldn't be joined together because of land restrictions, no matter the owners desire or how many lots the owner might own next to one another.

This left these mostly refurbished homes in Arlington and Southside as great starter homes. The area was close enough to the universities and local colleges that one could easily hop a bus or drive in ten minutes, with shopping all around, not to mention some of the best schools for kids in the southeast.

Turning on Darcey Street, Randy thought *"Those two areas would be a great location for us to start looking,"* then he spotted Catlin and pulled to the curb. "Hi," he offered as he quickly opened the door and helped her to lay out her things on the back seat.

"My meeting with Mr. Smith went better than I expected," he told her. "Get everything you need?"

"I think so," she told him as she got in and put her seat belt on. "Why did you put the top up?" she asked.

"I didn't want anything to get blown out the window or messed up by the wind," he explained.

It took about ten minutes to reach Randy's house. It was now 3 P.M., and Betty and Tamara were laying in wait as Randy and Catlin entered the front door.

Betty instructed her daughter to take the clothes Randy had been carrying up to her bedroom. Then took Catlin in tow, informing Randy to stay out of the way and in his own room until he was needed or called.

He knew better than to argue with either his mother or with three women, especially when he stood alone. *"Heck, even dad wouldn't attempt that,"* he said to himself as he took the hint and headed for his room to contemplate the fate that awaited him.

After waiting a very long time, Randy carried his white jacket over his arm and headed for the kitchen thinking he'd find his mother there with Catlin, as like many American families the kitchen is where most folks gathered, whether it's dinner time, or not. Most people believe it is the warmth associated with cooking, others feel it is the aroma of the spices that linger in the air. Either way, it is a fact that the kitchen is the gathering place that is always filled with love in this house.

One of the things Randy liked about his mother's kitchen was that there would always be fresh juice in the frig and coffee on the counter. "*I hope Catlin takes the hint and follows suit,*" he thought, or at least he hoped.

Going through the always opened bat-winged doors leading into the kitchen, he stopped, looking at those doors thinking, "I can't even remember seeing those doors closed," he said.

The kitchen was empty. "They must still be up stairs," he spoke softly as he opened the frig to take out some OJ, then laid his jacket over one of the chairs at the table and took down a clean glass and poured half a glass, leaving the balance sitting on the table, then sat down to wait.

❧

Chapter 5

Gone as time fell to
The rustle of leaves
Strength by the stones

Sitting there, Randy went over in his mind what he hoped would be all the right things and words he wanted to say. Or rather what he needed to say before the end of this day.

Suddenly, there was a noise in the living room and Randy stood and turned to go towards the sounds.

Entering the living room, he came to a sudden stop. Randy felt as though someone or something had knocked every bit of air from his lungs. He couldn't breathe and he was sure his heart was either going to explode or stop altogether. He wasn't sure what was happening, but before him stood three people.

Two he was sure he recognized, the third he was also sure he had never seen before. She appeared to be a princess. He thought he should bow but was not at all sure how one would bow to such loveliness.

The look on the young man's face touched the hearts of the three women before him and each smiled a special knowing smile.

"WOW!" was all Randy could utter.

Her hair seemed truly golden; done in a double-braid twisted into a six inch bun on either side of her temple. The tiara was silver and had the diamonds been real, its wealth could have paid off a very large portion of the national debt. Though delicate, it seemed to suit her face and sat well atop her regal head.

Her emerald eyes glistened with even the smallest of smiles. Catlin turned slowly around, allowing her Prince to fully examine a true work of beauty.

Randy found it difficult to take his eyes from her, even as she turned slowly around.

Directly behind her crown ran more than eight inches in width a flowing of her hair reaching deep down her back. The earrings were of pearl, to match the single strand about her long slender neck.

Drawn back to her face, every inch was pure, clean and barely touched by make-up. Her natural beauty was only highlighted by his mother's hand. Had his mother been a sculptress, she could not have made a more perfect image of beauty, at least not in his eyes.

If this was the woman he was to spend an eternity with, Randy was well pleased.

"You're not just beautiful, beauty cannot compare to the sight before me. You will steal the hearts of every boy at the prom tonight," he told her.

Randy hardly noticed his mother and sister standing on either side of Catlin until that moment. They both smiled. Neither could remember ever seeing Randy glow like this before, even when he woke up to find a shiny red Mustang convertible sitting in the drive with its big white bow.

This was a new page in the lives of the Carr family. *"Where has the time gone?"* Betty wondered.

"I'm gonna get the camera," Tamara told them, and headed for her father's desk.

Tamara, after returning with the camera, decided she needed to change, saying, "I don't want my picture taken in these jeans," then bounced back up the stairs.

Meanwhile, Betty took several pictures of both of them either coming down the stairs or on the bottom stair standing together.

It took Tamara less than five minutes before she returned wearing a pretty red dress with a white belt and matching shoes. "I didn't want to clash with your gown," she told Catlin as her mother took another dozen digital pictures on her new Cannon camera which she would

125

upload to her laptop later.

The time was now 4:50. "Dad's gonna hate that he missed y'all, but you'd best be going if you're going   to make your dinner reservation," Tamara reminded the young couple.

While leading Catlin towards the front door, Mary and the twins came in, "Wow!" the three of them said in unison. "You're prettier than Cinderella in our books," they told Catlin.

Doing a curtsy, Catlin said, "Why thank you. You can be my Princesses and my Fairy God Mother." Then she kissed each on the cheek before disappearing out the door with Randy in tow.

Remembering her fairy tales, Betty said, "Have a good time, but remember you have to be home by twelve," and they all had a good laugh.

It was before Randy pulled out of the driveway that Betty called after them. "Hey, you guys forget something?" as she held up two boxes; one a corsage, the other the carnation.

Betty had them stand next to the car as she pinned on both flowers of the night as the twins and Mary reminded all that they had not had their pictures taken with their new friend.

"We might be a little late," Catlin said, "but I think they will hold a table for us." Then she told Betty, "Go get your camera."

Five minutes later, they were on their way, having satisfied all but Randy Senior who they passed within a block of the house, tooting and waving as they headed towards downtown.

At Rudy's they had put on special attendants for parking the cars of the students and other guests they were expecting this evening, not only on Friday night, but a prom night.

There was already a long line of cars there when Randy told the attendant they had a 5:30 reservation, which put them at the very front of the line.

It took another twenty minutes before they were seated at a small and cozy table. The table cloth was linen and white. It held a small round red bowl with a white lit candle. The napkins were folded into the forms of swans at each of the two settings. The plates were off white with golden trim on the outsides. The silverware looked heavy, but was light to the touch.

Each setting had two crystal glasses, one of which held water, no ice. The other might be used for sodas or milk, he wasn't sure. Setting on each plate was a simple menu. The meal, minus tip, would run thirty to forty dollars each, pending drinks and desert.

Picking up her menu first, Catlin asked, "Can you afford this?"

"I've been saving for this one night for a whole year," Randy told her.

127

The waiter introduced himself, "My name is Curt." He was patient and offered them drinks and salads.

"Thanks," Randy said.

"There is a salad bar against the side wall," he said and then excused himself to get the Pepsi colas each had asked for.

Everywhere they looked, they saw kids their own age. "There must be over a hundred people in here and not a child in sight," Catlin said.

"Yeah," Randy agreed saying, "Everyone is dressed for some prom somewhere around the city."

Looking around the salad bar, they picked lettuce, tomatoes, cheese, croutons, cucumbers, and green bell peppers.

Heading back towards the table, Randy hadn't seen anyone for a while from the General, then found Steve and Wendy, but decided not to say anything to them since this was Catlin's special night out.

Holding the seat for Catlin at the table, the waiter came back with their drinks saying, "I'll give y'all a little time then come back for your orders."

Thanking him, they seated themselves to suddenly find several bottles of salad dressings in a tray centered on the table.

"What type of salad dressing do you like?" Randy asked.

"Ranch or olive oil mostly, but tonight, I think I'll have the Blue Cheese," Catlin said as she took the bottle out of the tray.

"My favorite," Randy said with a wide smile.

"Have you decided on what you want?" Randy asked.

"No, but I think I'm gonna have whatever you have, if that's alright with you," Catlin told him.

"I was thinking of having the butterfly shrimp with the cocktail sauce, then the rib-eye with mushrooms. How do you like your steak?" he asked her.

"Actually, I like mine a little well done, but not burned and I think I'll have the cheese instead of the mushrooms. Did you notice that they also have fried cheese and fried mushrooms?" Catlin suggested and then added, "I've never eaten fried cheese or the fried mushrooms. Are they as good as they sound?"

"They were great the last time we ate here. Just watch out for the centers because they can be very hot," he warned. "Either way, if you don't like them, I'll finish them for you."

"Okay then, that's what I'm having," Catlin told him satisfied with her own choice.

129

"The salad is good. Salads at home are always good but eating a salad in a restaurant seems to taste better for some reason. Just don't tell mom!" Randy teased her.

"Yeah, I feel the same way, and I've always wondered why. I mean, they're both fresh, using the same ingredients but it does taste better when eaten out," she concluded.

The main course came and went and the topic of the talk turned to Randy answering a few of Catlin's earlier questions of the day before.

"You asked if I can live without going to Law School or if you were worth giving up my dreams of becoming a lawyer. My answer to that much of your questions is yes, if I had to," he said. "I love computers and could become a computer programmer or a systems analyst. Given a choice, I'd rather become a corporate lawyer. They both work hard, put in a lot of long hours from time-to-time and the rewards are always worth it.

"As for having children," he went on, "I think every man and woman wants children of their own, but if we found we couldn't have any of our own, we could always adopt, unless you wanted a career, then it would be more your choice. An eternity with you will be worth most any sacrifice," he finished.

After hearing him out, Catlin took his hand and said, "I love you all the more for what you've said."

Holding her hand, Randy suddenly noticed that her hand was freezing and he asked "Why are you so cold? Your hands are as cold as death itself."

Then remembering the small box he carried in his breast pocket, he slipped it out and placed it in front of her as he got down on one knee while still holding her hand and said, "Catlin, a month ago, I didn't even know you. Today, I can't believe I haven't known you my entire life. You know how much I love you now, and I know that love can only continue to grow."

Opening the box, Randy said, "This ring was a small token of the love my grandfather had for my grandmother before her death. It was passed to me to share as a token of the love I'd have for one special person.

"Catlin, with all my heart, I love you and will forevermore. Will you accept this ring as a token of that love? Will you marry me?"

Still holding onto his hand, and seeing only him as he knelt before her, she allowed her tears to run down her face freely. Looking down and deep into his eyes, she suddenly felt, for the first time in her lifetime, that life would be worth living. "I found you in my heart the day our eyes first met," she said. "I knew you from the beginning of my life, yet only met you less than a month ago. You asked me to marry you? If it is within the powers to be, I would gladly be your wife. Either way, I will willingly spend my entire eternity loving you, and loving you always," she pronounced as Randy placed his grandmother's ring on Catlin's left hand.

Each had eyes only for the other, and heard only the whispers of the others until the clapping finally got their attention. When they finally took a breath, they found the maitre d' standing at their table.

"Sir, Madam," he began, "I have witnessed many a proposal in my life here during prom week, but I do believe the words spoken from your hearts, and seen through your eyes, will linger as the most promising of loves ever to come through our doors. Good luck and enjoy your prom night. In ten years, if your love is as strong as it is tonight, come back for a free dinner." Then he left the two to continue his duties.

Chapter 6

Alone as two, yet
Tied together as one
Through their love
Shared decades ago.

After their dinner, Randy and Catlin still had an hour to spend before they intended to reach the festivities in the General's gym.

"Let's walk down towards the Riverwalk," Randy said as they exited Rudy's.

"Okay," Catlin agreed.

The parking attendant started to retrieve the car when Randy asked, "Can we leave the car here for another hour? We'd like to take a little walk," as Randy handed the young man a five dollar bill.

"That's not necessary, sir," the attendant said trying to turn the tip down.

"It's alright, take it. We'll be back in about an hour," Randy explained.

The evening was beautiful as the day's sun was now nothing more than a purple hue in the western sky. The St. John's was quiet with its tide softly rippling towards the north.

Pointing, Catlin said, "There's the first star out tonight," as she took Randy's hand.

The only stars Randy could see were the ones reflecting off Catlin's eyes. Stopping suddenly, he spoke as he reached for her head, "Here, your tiara has shifted; let me straighten it for you."

Straightening and securing her delicate crown, he gently took her face into his hands and tenderly kissed her saying, "Catlin, I'm gonna feel cheated if I am only allowed to spend just a single eternity with you when there is so much more waiting for us."

Returning his kiss, she said, "An eternity is a long time. You might get bored or tired of me by then."

"Somehow," he said, "I don't think I could ever get tired of having you at my side."

Without thought, they stepped down the Riverwalk to its lowest level when a voice drew their attention, "Ten dollars for an evening cruise."

Glancing up, both were unprepared to see a beautiful golden gondola tied up to the pier.

The gondola was about thirty-five feet long and about eight feet wide at its center. At each end were two four foot poles housing lights of soft white.

Her gunwales were purple with gold trim; the bow pointed with a high arch. The square stern housed a rudder and what appeared to be an electric motor. Its interior was royal red with cushions of fluffy gold laid about its stern; the midship had what appeared to be a small table and a very tiny box next to it on one side.

Seeing where the young couple's eyes drifted, the driver stated, "I have Coke, Pepsi, and Dr. Pepper."

It was then they noticed a man of about twenty-five or so who had a guitar strung over his shoulder. It was a very beautiful instrument and was the same color as his boat.

"How long is the ride?" Catlin asked hopefully.

"About forty-five minutes, unless you want to ride further south," he offered. "That would take an extra hour and cost an extra twenty."

Looking at her eyes, Randy could see that special look he couldn't ever refuse, and he'd never tire of seeing, then said, "We've got just about forty-five minutes if we're gonna make the prom at a reasonable hour," and then he reached for his wallet and took out a crisp ten dollar bill.

The cabbie helped Catlin over the gunwale along a plank and into the flat bottom of the gondola. "It's safe, you can't tip her over," he spoke confidently as she sat down on one of the bright golden pillows.

"They're bean bags," he said with a nice smile.

"Thank you," they both said as Randy followed them and sat down on a purple pillow that was trimmed in the same gold as Catlin's.

"It's beautiful," Catlin exclaimed.

Agreeing, Randy asked, "Are you thirsty?"

"A little. We could share one," she offered.

"What would you like?" Randy asked as the gondola slipped out of her berth, the electric motor hum and as the water softly lapped the side of the boat in a rhythmtic tone.

Randy asked, "How much are the drinks?"

"Two dollars each and the chips are a dollar," he answered.

"We'll have a Dr. Pepper," Randy said as he opened the clean little box and extracted a 16 ounce bottle of cold Dr. Pepper, knowing he'd pay the man when they returned to the dock.

Laying back on her pillow, Catlin held up her left hand and said, "This is the most beautiful ring I've ever seen. Your grandfather must have loved your grandmother a lot. See how the lights of the city glitter off the diamonds?"

Laying down beside her, the entire world forgotten, Randy watched her and every little thing she was doing. "I guess he must have loved her nearly as much as I love you." Then their faces turned towards one another and he kissed her once, then again.

"Hey," the cabbie said. "You can't be rocking the boat."

Knowing what he meant, Randy and Catlin relented and lay back to enjoy the open skies, the brightening of the stars and the peacefulness of the ride.

Without offering, the cabbie swung his guitar around, tied off the rudder, and began softly strumming. He began to hum to the mood he felt around him, and the music just flowed freely.

It seemed that they had barely gotten themselves comfortable when the gondola touched her berth again. The cabbie, seeing the love and peace that had overcome the young couple and seeing there were no other customers in sight, played another song.

It was the closing song in the movie "Ghost", where Patrick Swayze held onto Demi Moore, gave her that last kiss, then turned and walked into the light.

As he played the last notes, he announced, "Sorry folks, we're back."

The young people stirred and looked about them.

"So soon," Catlin said with a sigh.

"Afraid so, other people are coming down the walk," the cabbie told them.

Being completely lost in the night stars and time, Randy took out a twenty dollar bill and asked, "Will you be here later tonight?" Looking at Catlin's lovely face, he said, "I think we might be back to try that longer cruise."

"I'll be here tonight until 2 A.M. Hopefully," he told them, "I'll see ya later," as he helped Catlin ashore. When finished, he started to give Randy his change, when Catlin put her hand over his and without questioning Randy first, said, "No, That's yours."

With a knowing understanding as to why, Randy said, "You've more than earned it." Then asked, "Tell us your name so we can tell our friends."

Reaching into his shirt pocket, he pulled out two business cards, handing one each to them saying, "My name is David Larmon,

I own the *Island Drifter*. My cell number and web page address are on it, but I'm usually here or down by the park most weekends. They can call for appointments and I'll meet them anywhere along the Riverwalk." Then thanked them as he returned to straighten up the pillows.

It was two blocks to Rudy's, and when they arrived, the attendant who had seen them approaching, pulled the Mustang up just as they got there.

Randy gave over ten dollars as a tip then headed for the General, arriving about eight-thirty, and parking the car in the student parking area, they then headed for the gym.

"Someone has done a lot of work," Randy said noting all the changes that had taken place since the two had left some eight hours earlier.

Farolitos had been laid out all along both sides of the sidewalk, creating a very romantic atmosphere and speakers had been placed in secluded areas allowing the music inside to be enjoyed almost any place on the school grounds, but the volume was down low enough not to disturb those living nearby.

"It's all so beautiful," Catlin said as she saw all the decorations that had been set out for prom night. "It's hard to believe they did all this since this afternoon."

"Wait until you see what they did to the gym," Randy told her as he led her towards the open doors to the main building, where they had set up a velvet rope to help keep the non-seniors out of the prom until they could attend properly.

"Good evening," a student usher spoke, "Do you have your Senior Prom pass?"

Bringing out his student I.D. card, Randy said, "This is my date, Catlin Hyde. She's a junior."

Pictures were taken of each couple prior to entering the building so they could be made available to the school's graduating class yearbook, and to those who wanted extra copies for themselves, which would only cost five bucks for their families and friends.

Some sixty feet down the hall was another set of doors, and another set of ushers, which held couples from entering the dance.

As they reached the main entrance, the couple in front of them gave the usher an index card they had received at the front door which held both names and graduation dates.

Once the cards were handed over to yet another usher, they heard over the loudspeaker an announcement. "Bryan Berryman, class of 2004 and his date for tonight is Carol Redkey class of 2003. We welcome you both.

"Mr. Berryman, an Honor Student and our third baseman, is wearing a black tux with a red cummerbund, white frilled shirt. and black tennis shoes.

Ms. Carol Redkey is a graduate of Terry Parker High and lead cheerleader for three years prior to her graduation last year. Her dark brown hair matches her eyes. Tonight, she is wearing a lovely gown of lavender with a matching sash to that of her bow."

As they stepped into the room, the music began to play *"Dance With Me"*.

Stepping forward, it was their turn. Taking her hand, he placed it over his arm and asked, "Are you ready?"

Catlin nodded and they stepped forward to be announced.

Looking up, the announcer who had been handed a card with their names and graduation dates took a moment to observe the pair and then took a second look and then looked again at his card and began.

The music died and the announcer, who was a classmate and friend, said, "The Honorable and soon to be attorney Randy Carr, class of 2004. He is dressed in a white tuxedo with long tails. He is trimmed in lime green striped trousers with matching shirt. He chose a ten inch cummerbund of royal pink to match his date's elegant dress."

"Catlin Hyde," he announced "a rare and beautiful crowned princess in the purest pink and purple silk, highlighted with the warmest creams of white, lavender and mauve. She's a junior, who I am sure will hold court over all those who attend her," the young man concluded as all eyes turned to see the most stunning girl in the room.

Most of the young men did a double take, and some took a third look at the beauty who held Randy Carr's arm.

141

The young women whispered amongst themselves asking, "Who is she?" While others asked, "Is she a real Crowned Princess?" A few remarked, "I've never seen her before," as others still commented, "I've never seen such a beautiful gown."

Then the music began anew with a new song: a country ballad called *"We Danced"*.

Randy had never been what one might call a true country music fan, but this song he loved. Although he never dreamed he would ever have the chance to do this in his lifetime, he led Catlin to the center of the dance floor. Neither seeing the other kids fall to the side as Randy took Catlin into his arms and began a slow dance.

Their moves were both graceful and so in tune with one another, many believed they had been dance partners for years. The crowd slowly began to trickle back onto the floor; first one or two couples then more joined in the dance as they too swayed to the soft music and were as caught up in the moment as were Randy and Catlin.

Looking deep into Catlin's eyes, Randy knew then as he had never known before, he said softly, "I love you!" as they continued to sway and move slowly around the dance floor.

Catlin's eyes never left his. She had no knowledge of those around them. "I love you too, and want to spend my entire eternity loving only you."

The dance lasted just under three minutes but for many whose eyes had been met with true love, the music seemed to last for three hours, a lifetime, and yet less than three seconds all at the same time.

For the first time this night, the song had not been interrupted by the announcer until its end when he announced the next couple.

When the dance was over, the crowd on the floor parted as Randy led Catlin to one of the small tables near a wall that was also lined with individual chairs for those who might not have a date.

From the moment Randy and Catlin had been announced, no one paid any attention to the couples who came in after them.

Within five minutes, the surface of the small round table they had sat at was teeming over with roses, carnations, and the most beautifully colored corsages either had ever seen, given to Catlin by dozens of boys and girls as a tribute.

One young man after another came up offering a drink and a few words of "Would you put me on your dance card?" The young women offering their hand and their names in hopes that later she might have a few moments of her time.

Neither had ever been so honored and so were truly taken aback. They had gracefully acknowledged each tribute with a warm hand shake and an honest, "Thank you!"

Two more songs had been played without any interruptions when Randy, forgetting himself, remembered and asked, "Are you thirsty? I could get you something to eat or drink."

"Thank you, but I'd really like another dance first," Catlin told him. "I didn't know you are such a good dancer."

"You can thank mom," he explained. "Dad couldn't dance a step during their whole time in school but when mom went with him to take dance lessons, I was about six and the dance instructor had a young daughter, and she taught me as her mother taught mom and dad."

No sooner had he completed his statement, he took her hand and headed for the hardwood floor, as the lights were dimmed way down low and a new oldie was just beginning. The song was *"Sixteen Candles"*.

Drawing Catlin close to him, she again forgot all about the dozens of people who had joined them on the floor; the strobe lights shining and glancing off its tiny mirrors to dance amongst those on the floor.

Again, a good song never lasts as long as the emotions of those embraced in it, and as it ended, Randy said, "I'll get us something while you hold the table," then he pointed her in the direction of the table that was full of flowers. I'll only be a couple of minutes," then she kissed him as he assured her and then he turned to the refreshment area on the far side of the gym.

About five minutes later, Randy wound through the crowds of kids looking for the table and Catlin. *"I must have gotten turned around,"* he thought to himself.

Randy circled the floor once again, then a third time before he scanned the dance floor, thinking one of the guys finally talked her into a dance, but he couldn't find Catlin anywhere.

After twenty minutes, Randy headed for the exit asking the attendant, "Do you remember the girl I was with?"

"Who didn't!" he responded. "How did you get so lucky, man?"

"I don't know, but have you seen her leave, maybe to go to the bathroom?" Randy suggested.

"No, man. I'd have seen her go. The restrooms are down the hall," pointing towards the large crowd standing in a line.

Going down the halls, Randy ran into Wendy. "I'm glad to see you," he said.

"Why, has something happened to Catlin?" Wendy jokingly asked.

"I went to get some refreshments and can't find her anywhere," Randy explained. "Would you mind checking the restrooms for me?"

145

"Okay, but I'm sure she's right where you left her," Wendy said as she backtracked to the girl's restroom.

Returning to Randy, Wendy said, "I'm sorry but she's not there and no one remembered seeing her. Let's go find this beauty before someone else picks her up and runs off with her."

Remembering that Catlin had another boyfriend, Randy was worried that perhaps he saw her with him and got jealous.

Returning to the gym, Randy took one side, Wendy the other. After looking for and inquiring after Catlin, no one had seen her since the second dance.

They both walked completely around the school yard and out to the football field, as well as the parking lot but she wasn't anywhere to be found.

Wendy, when she got back to Randy, said, "Did you say something to her to cause her to leave the dance by herself or with someone else?"

Randy, who had been racking his head over the same questions said, "Not that I can think of. She seemed more than happy and content to be with me."

"Well," Wendy said positively, "she couldn't just vanish into thin air, let's drive towards her house in case she started walking home."

Getting into Randy's car, Randy mentioned her old boyfriend, "Remember, I told you about Catlin's old boyfriend, a kid named Bobby Bargin?"

"Yeah," Wendy remembered and asked, "do you think she would have gone off with him without telling you or anyone else?"

"There must be a hundred places he could have taken her between the school and her house and we can't check them all."

"This just doesn't make any sense to me," Randy said flatly. "Why would she agree to marry me, saying she wouldn't want to spend her eternity with anyone else and then go off with someone she clearly doesn't love or want to be with without telling me first?"

Wendy said, "Let's look at all the open places before we jump off the bridge. I'm sure there is a logical explanation here somewhere," she told him, but deep down in the pit of her stomach, she had a cold, cold feeling for her friend.

"I'm gonna call Steve before he begins to worry where I got off to. I sure don't want him out looking for me while we're looking for Catlin," then took out her cell phone and using speed-dial, called Steve who was now, in fact, looking for her.

I was getting worried," Steve confessed. "Where are y'all?"

"We're heading towards Catlin's house. She disappeared during the

147

dance and Randy and I are trying to find her," Wendy explained.

"Need some help?" Steve offered. "It seems that my date ran off with another guy while I wasn't looking," he joked.

"Do you remember what she looks like?" Wendy asked.

"Yeah, sure. Everybody remembers her," Steve answered.

"How about you round up Frances and y'all check around the school for her. She might be with an old boyfriend named Bobby Bargin. Don't bother them, but if you find her, call me. I'll leave my phone on," she told him.

"OK, I know where Francis is. If she's here on campus, we'll find her and let you know," Steve assured her.

"Thanks," was all she said as Randy's car pulled into a local Burger King.

"I'll check the bathrooms while you go check the cars on the back parking lot," Wendy told him as she got out of the car at the side door.

"Gotcha," Randy said as he began to drive ever so slowly through the parking lot. *There's a lot of kids here from the General,"* he thought as he continued his search, up one side then back towards the front where he spied Wendy waiting for him.

"Not here, Bud!" she told him.

First it was the Burger King, then Jack-in-the Box, then Wendy's, then Micky D's. It was fast approaching midnight when Randy suggested, "Since we're already this close, I guess it wouldn't hurt to drive by her house. If the lights are on, I'll stop, if not, I'll take you back to Lee."

"Look," Randy said as Wendy finished a third call to Steve, "I'm really sorry I ruined your prom. I hope you and Steve will forgive me," he concluded.

"Randy, you're our friend. I think we'd both be hurt if you hadn't asked us to help. I know I'd want your help and support if the shoe was on the other foot," Wendy told him seriously.

"Steve said he and Frances are only blocks from the old Foremost Plant," she told Randy. "Why don't we meet at the Steak & Shake on King."

Down trodden, Randy agreed as Wendy called Steve again.

It was now 12:20am.

On the way, Randy thought to himself, *"there's a lot to be said for having such good friends."* It took them another ten minutes to reach the drive-in where Steve and Frances waited in his new Mazda.

"Let's go get something to drink," Wendy suggested. "Maybe we can

149

think of something between us we hadn't yet thought of."

As they sat there, Frances said. "You know the dance won't be over until, after two. Maybe, we should go back in case she came back while we were gone."

"She's right," Wendy told them. "Catlin might be there right now looking for you," and everyone agreed and they quickly left.

Only Frances rode with Randy back to the school. The other four rode in total silence, afraid to say something wrong.

Pulling back into the parking lot, they all headed for the gym, where they split up and searched every square inch of the buildings without finding any sign of Catlin, or finding anyone who'd seen her since she first got there.

"Let's check the grounds again," Steve and Wendy suggested.

"Okay," Randy said but not holding out much hope of ever seeing her again.

"Frances and I will take the stadium." The Robert E. Lee Football and Soccer Stadium would hold over twenty thousand eager football fans and while open during the day, it was closed after school hours. There were dozens of storage rooms and almost the same number of bathrooms. The search took them until 2:15 A.M.

The dance was clearly long over, the performers were taking down all the lights and wiring from the speakers as the janitorial crews began the removal of all the decorations from across the large school property.

Not seeing any police cars or squad car emergency lights, gave Randy hope that no dead bodies had been discovered anywhere on the school grounds.

After the search by Steve and Wendy, Frances and Randy, they met at the parking lot.

"We're sorry, Bud!" Wendy told Randy. "We must've asked two hundred kids, and nobody remembered seeing Catlin other than when y'all came in."

"The only thing I can think of is to wait until morning," Randy told them earnestly, "and then go to her house. Thanks guys! I'm sorry I've ruined your night," Randy told them.

Frances has already been reclaimed by her boyfriend, Ben who said, "It's only a dance and we'll have plenty of them in the future, and none of us have to go home anytime soon. We could go look again at the local hangouts."

"No," Randy said. "I'm gonna go home. I'll check on her in the morning, and let y'all know what happened on Monday."

Then they all split up, got in their cars and headed out.

ℭ

Randy felt his heart flutter as he pulled into the driveway at home. The lights were still on in the kitchen, but thankfully when he opened the kitchen door, he found it empty.

Turning the light out, he quietly climbed the stairs and went to bed. He did not want to talk to anyone.

ℭ

The alarm in Randy's head rang and rang again. Randy rarely used the clock's alarm to wake up by. He had his own internal clock to wake him before he needed to get up. This morning was no different only he didn't wanna see any of the family yet.

Slipping out of bed, he showered and shaved, then noticed his tux laying on the chair at his desk. He remembered when he picked it up, the clerk told him, "Be sure and check all the pockets, but don't dry clean it. We'd rather do that ourselves, and note any damage or stains on a note pinned to the front."

Not expecting to find anything, Randy began going through each of the pockets, but he did find something he'd almost forgot. On the inside jacket pocket was the ring box that carried the engagement ring he put on Catlin's third left finger. He had told her, "We might need to get it sized to fit your finger," explaining that the ring belonged to his grandmother that it might not be the right size and that I might have to take it to the jewelers. The ring fit like it had been made for her.

Remembering back to these special times he had seen and time spent with his grandmother he thought that Catlin and her were very nearly the same build, so it was little wonder the ring fit so well.

"Will she give the ring back?" he wondered. Randy hadn't slept a wink. He went over every little detail of the day's events in his mind and just couldn't find fault, even a little one that might have caused Catlin to bolt.

"Cold feet?" Sure he'd heard of people getting cold feet before an event, standing in front of a large crowd, or running away only moments before a wedding; but none of that fit the events of last evening.

As he came down the stairs, hoping not to see anyone, his mother was holding out two items to him. One, a large glass of Tamara's almost fresh-squeezed, ice-cold OJ and in the other, a steaming cup of Coffee. He knew he needed all three.

"From the look on your face, I'd say you had a rough night," Betty told her son, then led him to the kitchen where she sat him down at the table, refilling her own coffee cup and said, "Wanna tell me about it?"

153

"No!" was his first thought and answer, but Tamara's OJ did its job, as he said. "I don't know what went wrong. Everything was so right; then wham. Nothing wrong; nothing right. Just Nothing!"

"I don't understand," Betty said.

"Neither do I, Mom." Randy told her honestly. Then proceeded to tell her everything that took place after leaving the house the night before, leaving nothing out.

When he had finished, his mother shook her head in stunned disbelief, then asked, "So, what are your plans? And what if this other boy did take her away out of jealousy?"

"Honestly, Mom, I don't really know much of what I'm gonna do, or can do, even if she was forced to go with Bobby. I don't believe I can go to the police unless Catlin is willing to swear out a warrant, and I'm not sure that would be a wise idea either," Randy told her, then explained his thoughts.

"If Catlin were to swear out a warrant, he might be the type who gets physical and could turn on Catlin and her family. Remember, Mom, there have been all too many deaths caused by an angry and too jealous ex-boyfriend and or girlfriend."

Betty suggested, "Catlin has to make up her mind who she wants to be with and then break it off cleanly with the other. She's mature enough that she should be able to do so without having to put up with threats from this other boy."

"What I think I need to do today is go to her house. I need to know that she's alright," Randy told his mother. "Perhaps then she can tell me what happened. I thought I'd go over about ten so I'd better finish getting ready. I've also got to turn in my tux. They're gonna be open all day," he finished saying as he downed the last swallow of his sister's great tasting OJ.

"You want me to go with you?" Betty asked knowing things would have to be worked out between the two of them.

"No. This is something I've got to do on my own," Randy told his mother as he headed back up the stairs feeling just a tad bit better having talked things over with his best friend.

Ten minutes later, he was back downstairs and out the door. It was 9:05 A.M. the clock on the dashboard told him as he started the car.

It took him thirty minutes to turn in his tux and it was just after 10 A.M. when he pulled to the curb in front of Catlin's house.

Glancing around, there was no sign of life though there was one car still in the driveway.

Randy sat in his car for another ten minutes going over all the things he wanted to say to Catlin. "I just hope I'm doing the right thing," he

155

said as he finally stepped out of the car heading for the small, wood-framed house, walking up the thin walkway leading to the front door.

"At one time," he thought to himself, *"there must have been many beautiful flowers in the yard, but it must have been a long time ago."* Without realizing, he must have stood there another three or four minutes before he knocked politely on the long ago painted hardwood door. Once, then after a minute, he knocked twice more.

It was then that Randy first heard commotion just as the door finally, but slowly, opened.

The homeowner looked out the door at a young man of about eighteen or so. He was neatly dressed in denim jeans and a pocketless polo shirt. The shirt was white, and made his handsome face and light brown hair exceptional. He also noted that the visitor stood over him making him about six foot two or better, but not intimidating.

"I guess I must have looked about the same at his age," he thought to himself.

"Yes," the man said in a questioning manner, "can I help you?"

Randy had forgotten all about Catlin's parents, and hadn't given thoughts as to what to say to them should either open the door.

The elderly man at the door had to be nearing seventy years old, so to Randy's thinking, this man must be Catlin's grandfather or Great

156

Uncle.

"Excuse me." Randy started. "My name is Randy Carr. I'm looking for Catlin. Is she home?"

"Catlin who?" the man clearly was blank.

"Catlin Hyde," Randy said. "We go to high school together. I'm sure Catlin has told you about me."

"Son," the man said coldly, "my name is Michael Hyde and I don't find this a bit funny," as a voice came from within the living room.

"Who is it, Mike?" the female voice asked.

"Perhaps you are seeking another Catlin Hyde," the man offered.

"Sir," Randy insisted. "I've picked her up every day for school and dropped her off here every day after school so I'm sure I have the right address," he said with just a little touch of anger in his voice and mannerism.

The door opened further and an aging woman in a nurses uniform was suddenly standing next to the man as she asked again, "What does he want Michael?"

"He says he's looking for Catlin. 'Our Catlin,'" he told his wife.

"Maybe you'd better come in and explain yourself," Mr. Hyde directed as he and his wife stepped aside allowing Randy to enter the small quiet living room.

Randy had entered no more than a few feet when his eyes were waylaid by dozens of photographs of Catlin on walls, table tops and an array of pictures on an old piano.

Randy's eyes had not missed how each picture was in an old style picture frame and how each picture showed old, long-forgotten backgrounds of a 1961 Chevy, which was brand new, as still others showed Catlin, though a few years younger standing next to the car, which was itself parked in front of a then new house. *"This House,"* he realized.

The man and woman did not stop Randy as he went from picture frame to picture frame, picking up first one, then another, studying each, and gently setting each back where it had come from. The couple allowed Randy to continue this for a few more minutes, never knowing what he was seeing, not wanting to disturb the young man's thoughts.

It was then that Randy's eyes caught the likeness of another face he knew.

When Catlin had mentioned Bobby Bargin as her boyfriend, Randy had checked the school's records and found an old yearbook with Bobby Bargin's picture and the year he had graduated from the General.

In the picture he now held, was a picture of Bobby, but he wasn't standing alone next to the shiny Chevy. Standing next to him, with her arms around his waist, was Catlin. There was no mistake. They were both the same age and both properly dressed for the early 60's. The same clothing she was wearing the first day he had picked her up at the street corner.

"Do you know the boy in this picture?" Randy asked them.

"Yes," Mrs. Hyde said solemnly. "His name is Bobby. He was our daughter's boyfriend."

Setting the picture back where he took it from, and without asking or waiting, Randy and the Hydes sat down on a sofa that was old but still firm and comfortable.

Mr. Hyde sat at the left end and Mrs. Hyde sat at the right of Randy, having Randy between them. They sat there, each with their own thoughts for several more moments before Mr. Hyde said, "Son, what's this all about?"

Randy sat there for a moment more until Mrs. Hyde put her hand on his hands and said, "You came here looking for a girl named Catlin, is that right?"

Without realizing what he had done, Randy swallowed and nodded his head, then turning from one to the other, he simply and honestly said,

"I don't understand."

"What is it you are confused about?" Mrs. Hyde asked quietly. Then she said, "Our Catlin died in an accident in 1964. Yet, when I see you looking at her pictures, I can see in your eyes that perhaps in another time and life that you must have known her."

Looking at the woman, Randy suddenly felt tears rolling down his cheeks as he softly said, "I loved her more than life."

Patting his hand, Mrs. Hyde took pity on him and reached over to the coffee table and opened a well worn and preserved blue covered album.

For the next twenty minutes, Randy sat there as Mrs. Hyde showed him pictures of Catlin, not shown in the framed pictures around the living room.

Pictures of her at birth with baby foot prints and others as she grew into the young woman he came to know and love. Pigtails and pony tails to a freckled face and toothless six year old.

Randy looked and studied each phase of her all too short life. He never gave it much thought until then, but he had in fact known everything there was to know about Catlin Lynn Hyde as though he had lived his life with her.

Without knowing, but knowing nonetheless, he would see a ten year old Catlin standing behind her mother holding her fingers in a 'v' fashion behind her mother's head from the rung of a swing set and slide that had once been in the back yard of this very house, long before the shrubs had grown, or the small trees in these pictures had matured. This picture and others he knew too would be on the next pages of the album Mrs. Hyde was turning on the coffee table before them.

Before the album had had gone to where Catlin must have been twelve or thirteen, Mrs. Hyde asked him, "What do you know of our daughter?"

Randy began slowly, and left very little out of his tale. The next page of the album still hadn't been turned, though Mrs. Hyde held it in her lap with a hand holding it in its place.

For two long and loving hours, Randy told how his love for Catlin had grown in less than a single month. That he had vowed to Catlin a love that would last longer than an eternity.

For their part, the Hydes sat speechless and motionless at first, not believing the young man's story, then not wanting to believe it. Yet in their hearts, both saw the love this stranger had for a daughter now long dead and buried.

Randy, nearing the end of his story, stopped and took in a long breath and then said, "I can smell her scent as though she were sitting right

161

there in that chair."

What Randy couldn't and didn't know was that one chair he had pointed out was in fact the one chair Catlin had insisted on sitting in when she was alive. The Hydes looked at one another in total disbelief, knowing he could not have had any knowledge of such details.

Continuing through the album they came across Catlin's obituary, shown in the Florida Times Union and a list of those who attended her funeral. Bobby Bargin was a pallbearer, his picture showed his distress and pain for his loss.

The final pictures showed Catlin's burial plot and the simple white cross that stood over it.

"Where is she buried?" Randy asked. "I'd like to visit her."

"The Loving Hand of God Cemetery, off Blanding," Mr. Hyde told him.

'Would you like to go over there now with us?" Mrs. Hyde asked Randy.

"I think I have to," Randy answered. "That is, if it's not too much trouble."

"Son," Mrs. Hyde said. "I have never heard such a story in all my life, and wouldn't have believed it except for the love that is clearly in your heart and voice for our daughter. I feel you are as much a part of our daughter's life as either Michael or myself. As for myself," she continued, "if Catlin loved you as much as this girl you speak of did, then it means you are a very good person. What are you gonna tell your family and friends?" Mrs. Hyde asked, then offered a suggestion. "Why don't you bring your parents here tomorrow, say about noon for lunch, that way we can meet them.

"I'm not sure how I'll handle all of this," he told them truthfully.

"Perhaps it would be better if you, or we, tell them together," Mr. Hyde suggested.

"I don't know," Randy told them. "I'm not the type to hold things back from my parents."

"It's late, would you like to ask your mother over now, for a little lunch, then we can all go out to the cemetery together," Mrs. Hyde asked Randy.

"This is all so weird," Randy spoke his mind out loud. "I know this must be tearing both of you apart too," remembering these people were Catlin's parents and her only family, and he found himself caring as much for them and their feelings as he would his own.

"Let me call her. I know dad is out for the day, and my sister can watch the house and sit with my other sisters," he said as he took out his cell phone and remembered all the pictures of Catlin that were on his phone.

"I just remembered that I've got pictures of Catlin here on my cell phone. Would you like to see them?" he asked.

Now, this was something neither of them had expected. Randy then took his phone and they spent the next twenty minutes perusing all the pictures that had been stored. Each picture had a time and date assigned to them so the Hydes knew the pictures were current and of their daughter.

"My mother is a shutterbug and she has already loaded several dozen pictures to her lap top," Randy explained. "I think I can persuade mom to bring her lap top with her."

After looking at all the pictures on Randy's phone, they handed it back so he could call his mother. Both were in tears as they witnessed their long ago, dead daughter living in the present as though she had been reborn.

He hit the speed dial on his phone and Betty picked up. "Mom," Randy said, "Mr. and Mrs. Hyde would like to meet you for a little lunch, if you can get away."

"You mean right now?" Betty answered.

"Mom," Randy replied, "it's very important you come over here right now, and please come alone, but bring your lap top."

"I don't understand, Son. What's this all about?" Betty asked. "Is everything alright?"

"No!" Randy told her. "But I can't explain over the phone, just come over here," then gave her the address and directions.

"I'll be there in twenty minutes," Betty told him and then hung up.

When Betty drove up, Randy and the Hydes met her at the door. "Mom, this is Michael and Iris Hyde," he introduced them without telling her that these elderly people were in fact Catlin's parents.

Betty, for her part, at first thought like Randy that Catlin had been living with her grandparents. Then, she heard the most ridiculous story from Randy she'd ever heard. But, after reviewing all the evidence presented, she couldn't help but believe each word Randy had said. The evidence was overwhelming. "Catlin Hyde had died on May 10, 1964!" It was also a fact that the pictures that she had taken were of Catlin Hyde in 2004. Both sets of evidence were positive proof of both sets of circumstances.

"What now?" Betty asked as she helped Iris clear the small dinette table of lunch dishes.

"Mr. Hyde," Randy asked, "where did Catlin die?"

"According to the police report," which he withdrew out of a brown folder and handed him, "it says she died on the way to the hospital, but she was hit by the car at the school bus stop at the corner of Edgewood and Roosevelt, just a few feet from the railroad tracks.

"This is too weird," Randy thought and then said, "The same spot I met her at and began picking her up from everyday."

"This becomes more incredible with everything we learn," Betty agreed. "But now, I mean, after all these years, why did she return now instead of years ago?" Betty wondered aloud.

"I don't know, Mom. I can't figure it out. But I've got another question even more important: will she be at that bus stop on Monday?" Randy pondered outloud.

"Would you stop and pick her up if she were?" Iris asked.

"God," Randy answered. "I just don't know," he said honestly. "I really don't know, and if I did, what then?"

Iris had a morbid thought, "Could we get our daughter back after all these years? Oh God, what then?"

Michael suggested, "We were gonna go to the cemetery this afternoon. Would y'all like to go with us?"

"Yeah," Randy had already told them that he intended to go but then asked Betty if she'd like to go, too.

"I feel like I have to go," Betty told them.

Betty left her car at the curb behind Randy's in front of the Hyde's house and almost left her lap top and Cannon there as well, but remembered at the last moment.

The drive to Blanding Boulevard was short and the four people in the Toyota held their own counsel.

The Hydes out of habit always brought with them their family album, and today Iris held it even more tightly than she had during the ride to visit their only child's grave site during the last forty years.

When Roosevelt branched off to the left at Blanding, there was a small strip shopping center to their immediate right, and today Michael pulled in and parked in front of a small flower shop where he explained, "Iris and I always stop here and buy six white roses." The roses they would always place on Catlin's grave.

Randy and Betty had gone in with them, each thinking they, too, would like to buy something special for Catlin, but after looking through the coolers and specials, neither found anything they liked or thought Catlin might like.

Leaving the flower shop, they drove less than a mile when Michael turned into the National Cemetery. Driving through the open gates, they approached a little chapel where all four got out and said prayers.

Getting back into the car, they drove up the winding road to a corner where the ground rose. They pulled over near several benches and a water fountain. They left the car and walked up a trail where there stood several rows of stones. It was then that each had thought they saw her white cross.

Looking, Iris and Michael were floored. This was not the cross they had seen every weekend for the last forty years, though the ground remained unbroken.

Approaching the grave, the second thing they all took notice of was there atop her grave, dozens of flowers, all fresh, and amongst them was the distinct corsage Betty had pinned on Catlin only the night before.

It was only then that Randy noticed that this cross was different than the one in the family album the Hydes had shown him, and he recognized why. The cross in the pictures showed Catlin's cross to be solidly built out of white granite; whereas, the one before them had an opening just below the solid tee section that now was opened clean through, liken to a window.

In the heart of the opening stood a clear crystal vase, secured by its base which looked like it might slide out of its holding grooves, yet when Randy tried, the vase would not move. In the vase, was the single bright yellow rose Randy had given Catlin the morning before, on their way to school.

"I remember her saying to me," Randy told them softly, "I love it so much," he said that she finished with, "I'll take it to my grave."

When Michael tried to remove the single rose, his fingers passed right through it and as hard as he tried, he could not touch the petals of the rose, even though his eyes told him it was there, it seemed as though it were just a mirage; seen but untouchable.

Randy and Iris knelt by the grave, Betty and Michael stood there in their own thoughts, perhaps in prayer or perhaps just lost in some memory. They remained there for some time, and Betty silently took pictures that she later would upload to her lap top.

As they left the grave site, Mike and Iris told them, "We need a few minutes in the chapel. We won't be long," then it was just Betty and Randy in the car.

"What are we gonna tell the girls," Betty asked?

"I don't know," Randy said and then asked, "What do you make of all of this?"

"To be honest, I halfway expected a camera crew ready and waiting to jump from behind a building or tree with Allan Funt saying, *Gotcha*!" Betty told him.

169

When they were all in the car heading back to the Hyde's house, Michael had a thought. "You asked earlier, why now, after all these years? Perhaps she returned many times, but only this time found the love she searched for in Randy."

"Or, perhaps she waited until now for some other reason," Iris offered. "I guess we'll never know," she concluded.

"What do we do if she is standing at that bus stop on Monday?" Randy asked. "What am I supposed to do and/or say to her? Should I bring her here, or question her as to her death?"

"Randy," Iris said after some thought, "no, don't bring her here, at least not yet."

Randy thought out loud, *"God! I don't know what to do."*

Putting her hand on his, Betty said, "None of us know what to tell you. We're all here if she comes back. Neither of you will ever be alone, and we'll figure something out should she return."

There was agreement all around.

Fifteen minutes later, they pulled in the driveway on Darcey Street, and while standing in the front yard of the house, they said their goodbyes with a promise that they would forever be in touch with the other in the future.

Randy followed his mother home wondering what they'd tell the rest of the family. When they got home, everyone was curious. But, after seeing Randy go upstairs without so much as a word, and expecting to see some sort of joy from their brother over his engagement, they knew something had happened. They did not know how severe it was, only that it must be something very bad.

When the kids approached their mother, she too was very somber in her actions, saying only that one needed time to think. Sensing something was wrong, each of the kids retreated to their rooms, knowing nothing and trusting in their parents to tell them what was wrong.

Randy Senior came home to an all too quiet house – a house normally filled with lively children running all over the place, especially when they heard him come home.

After checking the lower house and not finding anyone in the family room or the kitchen, he quickly became worried and headed upstairs where he opened the doors to each of his children's rooms checking on each to ensure they were okay.

Seeing each child, and the mood they were in, he knew something was very wrong. *"But what?"* he asked himself. Perhaps someone other than Betty or the kids. "Catlin? Oh God, I hope not," remembering when he had heard about "his" Catlin all those years ago.

171

Half an hour after Randy Senior got home, Betty sat quietly in her darkened bedroom and he sat down beside her and asked, "What's happened?"

Without answering him, she stood and excused herself, leaving him sitting in the   room and walked down the short hallway to Randy's room where she knocked on the door twice, then opened the door and asked, "Can we talk?"

Still quiet and looking lost, Randy pulled up a chair for her and she sat down.

"I think," she said, "we'd better tell them the truth. They are gonna know something is wrong and neither of us are very good at hiding our feelings and emotions."

"But," Randy started to say, "how can we explain it? Especially when we can't explain it to ourselves."

Thinking, "Why don't we simply state the truth about what we know?" Betty suggested.

"That being?" Randy again looked lost.

"That Catlin was killed in an accident when she was hit by a car. We don't have to mention that it happened forty years ago," Betty explained.

"Mom," Randy asked, "What if Catlin is waiting at the bus stop come Monday and what if she's waiting for me to pick her up like nothing has happened?"

Thinking, Betty made one final suggestion. "I think for tonight and this weekend, what we'd better say is that she's been in an accident and that we simply don't know anything more yet."

"What about dad?" Randy asked.

"Same thing, I guess, at least until we know more next week. We need to see what happens, then we can tell him everything," she suggested.

After their talk, Betty thought better of than going back to her bedroom and headed for the kitchen where she fixed a simple Hamburger Helper and called the family to dinner.

After a solemn dinner, Betty said to her brood, 'There's been an accident."

Everyone seemed to know it involved Catlin due to Randy's demeanor.

Tamara spoke the words, "It's Catlin, isn't it?'

Randy had tears in his eyes as his mother said, "Yes."

Mary and her father asked, "Is she going to be okay? Is there anything we can do?"

"We spent the day with her parents, we're all at a loss for what to say or do. When we know more, we'll let you know. Right now," Betty suggested, "the best we can do is pray, each to his or her own God and in their own way."

♋

Sunday came and went with little fanfare. Wendy called and Betty told her the same story and then begged off until they knew more.

Monday morning started off normal enough until Randy came down the stairs looking like death warmed over at the wrong temperature.

"You aren't going to school looking like that are you?" Betty asked.

It was 6:30 A.M.

"Mom, I guess not," he offered, but didn't seem all too sure that he knew or wanted to do anything about it, but old habits, even good ones, have a way of taking over when the body and or mind takes a little time off. "I'll be down in a few minutes," and then went back upstairs.

Presentable, Betty made Randy eat, though she couldn't make him sit for a full breakfast. He did manage a small helping of scrambled eggs and some dry toast with a cup of coffee and a glass of OJ.

174

"Look," Betty told Randy, now that they were alone. "You've got to know! All of us need to know! I'd go with you, but I don't think that would help."

"I know, Mom," Randy told her. "I'm not sure I will know what to say or do if she's standing there again. How do I react? Just wave at her and drive on by?" he asked.

"I don't know the answer, Son, but you need to know first if she is there; second, if she is there, you'll want to know, and deserve to know, why has this happened now, and more importantly, to you. And what she expects to happen next?" Betty told him, then concluded with, "Son, I know how hard this has been on you, but you'll never know until you go over there." Then kissed him on the forehead and escorted him out the door saying, "Call me when you know more," and turned away as he got in the car.

Randy at first thought he'd leave the top up, but the weather was just too perfect, cool, and bright. There was just the right amount of a late spring breeze, that leaving the top up would be an insult to owning a convertible. So, in less than a minute, the top was down and he was backing out of the driveway.

Turning off of Edgewood, there were any number of directions he could go to reach the General, Edgewood to Roosevelt was only one. Randy gave thought to every other direction in his mind, but his

175

mother's words kept coming back to him. *"You need to know."* and like most mothers, she was right as usual.

"I do deserve to know," he said aloud then he started to get mad. *"Damn it. I have to know,"* and then headed for the bus stop. The time was now 7:35 A.M.

Passing McDonald's, Randy continued another two blocks where he saw the Duncan Donuts on his right. Without thinking, he pulled in, got out and went inside.

"I'll have four twisted glazed, two large orange juices, and two coffees black, cream and sugar on the side, please," he told the girl behind the counter.

The waitress was strikingly beautiful. She might have been eighteen, certainly not more than twenty. Her black hair glistened, and she wore it in a single ponytail, which she wore a hairnet over. Randy remembered thinking that she must be part German because he had only seen her hair color on women who were of German descent.

Randy wasn't really looking at her; his mind was on whether Catlin would be there waiting for him, but the girl was beautiful, and he was still a man.

After paying his bill, he took the food to the car and placed it in the back seat holders, got in and headed for the bus stop.

The time was 7:48. At exactly 7:55 A.M., Randy hit the corner of Edgewood at Roosevelt Boulevard. The light was green and glancing to where Catlin normally would be waiting for him, he did not see anyone.

Randy decided he would give her a few more minutes and pulled over to the curb.

"Whew!" the voice came from the rear of the car, as Randy heard the familiar voice say, "I'm glad you pulled over."

Randy's heart almost stopped as the passenger's door opened and the voice got in and put the seat belt on.

Without saying a word, Randy pulled out as the light turned green. He made the left turn and pulled into traffic.

"Man, I thought I was gonna have to walk to school," John Phillip told him. "My car just died right there at the theater."

Still looking in the two rear view mirrors, Randy hoped against hope he would see some sign of Catlin. "Damn!" he said out loud.

"What?" John Phillip said in answer.

"No, it's not you," Randy said. "I was hoping to meet my girl there at the corner. I guess she's still mad about something."

"Oh yeah, man, I remember now. Isn't she the one who walked out on you during the prom?" John Phillip asked.

"No-o-o, she didn't walk out on me. Something happened and I haven't been able to talk to her since."

"Bummer, dude," John Phillip said sitting back in the seat.

Randy drove on to the school, the food and drinks in the back seat forgotten.

"Thanks, Randy," John Phillip said. "I really do appreciate the ride. I hope things work out between you and your girl," and then got out and disappeared into a group of students.

Putting the top up, Randy found the donuts and the OJ. He threw the coffee away and downed two of the twisted donuts and washed them down with the orange juice and headed for class with a long glazed twisted donut hanging out of his mouth.

The rules pertaining to cell phones in school are simple. If you have a phone, it must be turned off when on school grounds, even in the student parking areas, and since the first bell had already rung, Randy would have to either get permission to call home from the office, or wait until after school to tell his mother what took place at the bus stop.

Getting out of school at one o'clock, Randy headed home. It was then that Randy told his mother about what had taken place at the bus stop. "I thought I was gonna jump clean out of my skin when I first heard the voice before I realized it belong to someone else from school in my Homeroom class.

"I'll bet," Betty replied.

"What now?" Randy asked. "We've got to tell the family the truth, or something." He finished with, "I don't like lying."

"I've been giving it some thought," Betty offered. "The kids are old enough to understand life and death, but they would never understand her death being forty years ago. Even after seeing all of her pictures and her parents, it is still hard for me to believe." she told him. "I know how hard all of this has been on you. How are you holding up?" Betty wanted to know.

"Better than I have a right to," Randy confessed.

"Alright then," Betty finally said after giving her thoughts a few more minutes to sink in. "Here's what we're gonna do," she explained, and not seeing or knowing of a better idea, Randy agreed.

That evening after dinner, Betty took the lead in telling her daughters that Catlin had died while waiting for the bus.

While Randy Carr Senior had already been told the truth, he couldn't help reliving his past. Remembering how he first felt when he first met

179

his son's date, only to find out that she was in fact the same girl of his younger dreams.

Mr. and Mrs. Hyde had Catlin's last yearbook from the General. Randy remembered that Catlin had not been in any of his classes, but they did have contact throughout their daily activities, but as stated before, Catlin had eyes only for her Bobby.

Randy had known Bobby Bargin and very much liked the tall, lanky young man. Bobby was two years older than he was and was to graduate with honors.

During several of their school's and community science fairs, Bobby's entries won several honors, along with a very hefty scholarship. He was sought after by many major developers with promises of grandeur.

While it was only a few months after Catlin's death, he finally decided on a job with a west coast firm that specialized in earthquake proof structures.

After college, he heard that Bobby moved west, it was told that he felt there were just too many ghosts haunting him here in Jacksonville.

Randy never heard of him getting married, and had always wondered if he had.

Randy had known where Catlin had been buried and had actually visited her grave once, placing a single white rose on it before leaving.

Catlin was the only girl of his dreams that seemed to linger in his mind's memory long after all the other girls had faded away.

Randy Carr had never told his wife of his secret yearnings…after all, Betty had always been there for him. "His Rock!" His friend, and even before Catlin had come along, Betty had been his only lover. She did not then or now need to know or hear of his youthful fantasies for another girl who was now dead.

This certainly was not the time to bring it up. "*No,*" he thought to himself, "*This was something he would keep to himself.*"

After dinner, Betty took each of her daughters aside and told them. There were many tears because it seemed that everyone really liked Catlin, and all wanted things to work out for their brother. Catlin just seemed to fit in as a part of their family. There were a lot of tears and sobs, and it took Randy, his mother and father, to console each and get them into bed early. Sleep is a soothing comfort when grieving.

Randy did not go to work that day, or the next; and when he did, Wendy and the Smith Law firm had already been told by Betty of Catlin's death, so they went easy around Randy.

It was Tamara who suggested to Randy to place a cross at the bus stop where Catlin had died, and Betty agreed that it would be a good beginning to his healing, so he found a stone cross maker and ordered a simple white cross that the city would allow him to place without needing a permit.

When the marker was completed, Randy and his mother drove to pick it up. That Sunday, Randy woke up, and after having a small breakfast of corn flakes, he rummaged through the garage and found his father's garden tools.

Taking the small hand-held spade, Randy put Catlin's cross in the trunk of his car and kissed his mother and sister who wanted to go with him saying, "This is something I need to do alone." Then climbed in the car and backed into the street.

It wasn't long after leaving the house that Randy did two things. First, he drove over to the Hyde's house and told them what he was gonna do, and showed them the white cross he had purchased.

"It's beautiful, Randy," Mrs. Hyde told him. "I feel sure she would love your doing this for her."

"You truly must have loved her," Mr. Hyde told Randy, "if you are willing to put yourself through so much pain and suffering in putting a cross at the spot she died."

"Son," Mrs. Hyde asked, "do you really know where that spot was?"

"I think so," Randy explained. "I think it has to be the exact spot I first saw her standing at the curb where the records, say a school bus stop used to be.

"I had a little time to check the records of both the police and the EMT's files that took her to the hospital. So I'm pretty sure it'll be close. I feel it will be close enough to where anyone walking or driving by will be reminded of the precious life that was taken by someone who was distracted while driving, and I hope it might remind us all to pay more attention when behind the wheel of a car."

Taking her husband's arm with her hand, Mrs. Hyde said, "I hope so," then kissed Randy on the cheek, and he caught just the slightest whiff of a scent he knew he would never forget; a scent that could have belonged to no one else except for Catlin or her mother. A scent he would search for, for an eternity.

Randy bid them well and got back into the car remembering one other thing he felt he needed to finish.

Driving down Roosevelt, Randy peered over at the bus stop as he passed Edgewood, he guessed to himself, hoping, but not seeing the lone figure of the girl he had pledged his eternal love to and for knowing in his heart he'd never see her again in this lifetime.

As he passed by the old Foremost Dairy processing plant, he wondered again why the old plant and land had never been redeveloped. "*A question for Mr. Smith perhaps,*" he mused.

As the thought passed, he turned, heading for the General, or to where the little church was.

183

Not remembering ever seeing the church before, he just went to the student parking lot area, then drove around each block, adding one block to the square, thinking he'd find it eventually.

When he had covered more than two dozen blocks, he drove back to the General. When he got within two blocks of the school, he saw the church sitting there on the corner and wondered *"How that could be, I've been by this corner over a thousand times, and just drove by it four more times and still didn't see it, yet here it is!"*

Randy parked the car and approached the front doors wondering if he would find them opened to him once more, and if its pastor was there. The doors were unlocked and he entered to find Pastor Snowden at the front of the church near the altar.

Walking in, Randy saw the pastor turn around and seeing the young man, smiled as he waited for Randy to approach then put out his hand in welcome. "Well, how are you today?"

"Pastor Snowden, sir." Randy said, "I really need someone to talk to and perhaps a little advice," Randy told him, still unsure what advice he needed.

"Wanna Pepsi?" the pastor asked as he led Randy back towards his office.

℘

After spending nearly an hour at the church where Randy just felt a need to tell this stranger everything, he left feeling better about himself and what he was about to do. He also had a better understanding of the loss he felt in his heart and life.

"It's as though," Pastor Snowden told him, "you were already married to Catlin and suddenly she died. Her death, whether it was forty years ago, or seven days ago really changes little. You are the one left alive and will always wonder, 'Why me? Why here? And, why now, after all these years?' But Randy, I'm afraid that the only one who can answer those questions is God himself. We're only mortals, we can't see or understand what God ordered for us. We just have to trust in him and know in our hearts that whatever God has in store for us is in our best interest. Perhaps this will help you, son; I'm sure I haven't got the right answers you seek, but maybe I've helped some," Pastor Snowden finished.

It didn't take long after leaving the little church behind that Randy did realize he was more at peace with himself than he'd ever been in his life. "Thank you God" was the only real coherent thought he'd had in a long time.

Retracing his steps, Randy drove back to Edgewood and parked the car near the old bus stop next to the theater in front of the Toy's R Us, and removed the cross and his father's spade, carrying them to the area he felt the strongest was where Catlin had died almost forty years before,

185

and again only seven days before.

He stood there a long time lost in thought, then knelt down setting both of his burdens on the ground and returned to the car for the last item.

He had used Quick Crete before to repair a broken area in the sidewalk in front of their house last year and knew that it set up quickly and wouldn't let go of whatever was planted in it. While it only weighed five pounds, for some reason this morning it seemed to weigh a ton.

His only thoughts were of Catlin and how much he missed her. He thought he could still smell her scent lingering right there as though she were standing right over his shoulder. Randy almost turned, but knew it couldn't be her.

The hole he dug was almost ten inches in diameter; then he dug down about eighteen inches. The stone engraver marked the stone saying "If you don't plant it to the mark, a high wind or lawn mower bumping into it could knock it over, and any lower will make it look off." So Randy followed the instructions and then added the wet bag of concrete he had brought, mixing it as he half filled the hole before sliding the cross into the hole and tapping it into place at the mark. He held it in place allowing the concrete to harden somewhat.

Randy Carr knelt there holding the cross of the girl he had pledged his love for, oblivious to all the commotion going behind his back.

There was a sudden screech of tires that at first sounded surreal to his clouded mind. By the time he had realized what was happening and was trying to turn, Randy Carr never saw or felt what had hit him. His last thoughts were of the scent of Catlin Hyde. A scent he would take to his grave.

ॐ

Chapter 7

Weeping for the child
Whose heart was pure
Into this cruel world
He had an all too short a
Lifetime to endure it all.

Betty Carr was at home when her land line telephone rang, an occurrence that hadn't happened in what seemed like since she learned of her father's sudden death from the local police department. "Hello," she answered as she picked up the receiver.

Answering the phone, the words she heard were as cold as the ones announcing her father's death. "Mrs. Betty Jean Carr?" the voice asked.

Betty's heart, mind, and body suddenly turned to ice as she tried at first not to think, and was more afraid to say a word.

The voice spoke once more, shooting icicles straight through her mind.

"Yes," she stumbled with the words, "Yes, I'm Betty Carr."

"Ma'am," it was the voice of a man based on the few words she actually heard, she thought he must be in his fifties.

"I'm Lieutenant Bryan Berryman with the Duval County Sheriff's Office. You have a son named Randy Carr, Junior?" It was more a statement than a question.

Tamara was in the kitchen with her mother when the call came in. Seeing the shocked look on her mother's face, she yelled, "Daddy!" and reached to steady her mother as Betty Carr dropped the receiver to the counter top. "Dad!" she screamed again.

Running into the kitchen, Randy tried to take in what was happening. At first, he saw nothing more than Tamara pointing to the phone and holding her mother who was in tears. It was then that he vaguely remembered hearing the telephone as it rang earlier, then he saw the phone receiver sitting on the counter and picked it up.

He hadn't said a word as the voice was saying something, but he hadn't heard it all. "I am sorry," Randy Carr said into the phone. "What are you saying?"

Randy listened intensely as he was being told that both he and his wife were needed at the Edgewood Memorial Hospital as soon as they could get there because Randy Carr Junior had been involved in an accident. The man said to go straight to the emergency room and ask for Doctor Jerry Mobley, and that he would meet them there.

"Is he . . . ," Randy's voice froze in his throat.

"I don't know, Mr. Carr. Just hurry!" the Lieutenant told him. After explaining what he was told to Tamara and Mary who had also entered the kitchen.

Randy Carr took his wife and headed upstairs to get their cell phones and other papers they were told to bring and were out the door in under three minutes with a promise that he would call once they got to the hospital.

"My God!" Betty said as she sat next to Randy Senior in the car as they sped towards the unknown fate that awaited them and their only son. "I mean, it's only been ten days since Catlin," she couldn't finish the words, "and now Randy!"

"Honey," Randy said taking her hand, "we don't know anything yet. Let's just hope for the best. The Lieutenant wouldn't tell me anything."

"I know," she said, "but you don't suppose that Catlin came back to claim Randy knowing that he's gonna fall in love with her?"

It took all of twelve minutes to get to the Edgewood Memorial Hospital. When they arrived, there were several Police cars, two of which still had their flashing lights on and literally blocked the rear entrance to the emergency exit doors.

Finding a parking spot just past the entrance, they parked and quickly headed back to the emergency room per instructions.

Going through the extra wide double doors, their senses were met with mass confusion as police, doctors, nurses, patients, parents, and crying children seemed to be running amuck.

Seeing a single person, a male nurse sitting behind a desk, they approached him. "We were told by a Lieutenant Bryan Berryman to come to the emergency room and ask for Dr. Mobley. My name is Randy Carr, Senior. This is my wife Betty Carr. It's our son!" he finished.

Without preamble, the nurse excused himself and quickly walked to a plain-clothed man of about fifty or fifty-five who was dressed in a dull grey suit. The nurse pointed towards his desk and the nervous couple standing in front of it. They waited a few minutes and two men joined them.

One was clearly a doctor or another nurse, the other was wearing a deep steel blue suit. He didn't seem to be a police officer, and didn't stand like a doctor or nurse. The four approached the Carrs.

Pointing, the doctor before trying to introduce himself quietly suggested, "Perhaps we'd better go in here," again pointing to what appeared to be a simple and small chapel just off the emergency room. They allowed themselves to be led inside.

They were offered seats and sat down.

The Lieutenant took the lead and introduced each person to the Carrs. "I'm Lieutenant Bryan Berryman," handing each one of his Official Business cards, then introduced Doctor Charles English. "I'm the head of Emergency Trauma Medicine," he explained. "I'm sorry, we did everything we could."

All the other words were completely and totally lost to both Betty and Randy. Their lives completely shattered with the two simple words "I'm Sorry,"

Randy instinctively took Betty into an embrace, holding her closer than he could ever remember holding her, trying to not hear any other words, yet, needing to hear everything being said.

Doctor English was saying, "There was just too much trauma to his chest. We couldn't keep his heart going. We've got him on life support, but I can't see it helping for long. There is just too much damage. I checked his lungs. One is good, the other is beyond repair and is collapsed. His liver and kidneys seem okay, but we're still waiting for the test to come back. His heart is so damaged, he can't last long without a replacement, and the nearest heart is in Miami, and he won't last long enough even if there's a match. Again, I'm truly sorry," he offered.

It was at that moment that another med tech walked up and handed the doctor some papers. He turned to the Carrs and announced, the tests are in, his left lung is gone, and there's internal bleeding, and I know for sure that his heart couldn't take the strain of an operation, but I do have a team waiting if that's what you want."

It was less of a question than a statement, leaving the Carrs with a choice to make.

After giving it some thought, Randy Carr turned to the doctor and said, "Doctor, our son has repeatedly told us that should something like this ever happen to him that he wanted to be a donor. Can any of his organs be used for that purpose?"

"Mr. Carr", Doctor Berryman stated, "here in the Jacksonville area alone, there are some two thousand people in need of a donor."

It was then that the Lieutenant handed Randy a card saying, "I found this in your son's wallet, but I have to let you make the choice." The card was Randy Junior's "Donor Card" attached to his Florida Drivers License.

"Brain waves", Betty almost shouted. "I've heard that he might be alright if he still had brain waves," she cried, not wanting to give up her only son.

"True," the doctor said agreeing, "and there are some, but they seem sporadic at best, but nothing to indicate real brain activities that might give us hope for any kind of recovery."

"I want to wait," Betty said. "He might just be in some kind of trauma type coma. Let's give him every chance to come back to us."

"We can give him eight to twelve hours," Doctor English told them, "anything past that point, and the fact that there is such a weakness in his heart, his other organs will deteriorate quickly and might not be usable as donor transplants. But that choice is yours to make."

"So cold! So emotionless!" Betty thought of the doctors words, but in her heart, she knew her son had already passed from this life, and she cried again as Randy held her ever closer.

Holding tightly onto her husband, Betty looked up into his gray eyes hoping to find some spark of hope in them.

"We'll give him every second we can, but we'll have to know by," and the doctor looked at his watch and said, "By 3 A.M. so we can line up those who are waiting for a donor." He went on to say, "It'll give us time to do a complete check and breakdown of tissue samples before and will give the recipients the best chance for a successful transplant and a speedier recovery."

"Is there anything we can do?" Randy asked the doctor.

"Pray is the only true help. It's all up to the boy and his God," Doctor English told them as a third person entered the room.

"This is Pastor Hank Snowden; we found his card in your son's shirt pocket and called him," Lieutenant Berryman told them.

Shaking their hands, Pastor Snowden had Randy's parents sit down in a pew and told them of his knowledge and the friendship that he had with their son.

"We've not attended any church in years," Randy said in answer. "We're glad you're here and even more so because you know Randy. I don't think we'll be able to handle all of this without some help."

"I'm sorry, Mr. Carr," a female voice broke in. "We need you to sign some papers before we move your son to a private room. Do you have any insurance?" she asked. "We'll need the policy number for our records."

Randy pulled out his wallet, handing the woman in white a small business card saying, "The info is on the backside. You can call Jim Henderson, he's our agent; he can tell you what you need to know."

Turning, Randy saw his wife kneeling to pray with Pastor Snowden, then joined them, praying for the first time in many years openly in a chapel.

Lieutenant Berryman came back in half-an-hour later holding four cups of coffee from Micky D's. "The coffee in the hospital is always terrible so I thought you'd appreciate a decent cup. There's cream and sugar in the bottom of the tray."

Then, he told the Carrs everything he knew of the accident that might still claim their son's life.

"The driver," Lieutenant Berryman said, "was driving a new Buick, when several things seemed to happen at the same time causing him to miss the brake pedal and stomp on the gas, trying to miss a child that darted out from behind two cars. Then another car from across the road backed out causing him to swerve into your son. I can't see any way the driver could have done anything to prevent the accident. We're taking blood samples to be sure, but at this point, I can't see any charges being filed. The man's name is Petersen. He's already donated two pints of blood to your son. I think it might ease his mind if he could talk to you later, that is, if you're up to it."

"No, I don't think this is the best time for that," Randy said.

"That's okay. I'm sure he will understand," Berryman agreed. "He just wanted you to know he'd do anything, including donating his own heart to bring your son back."

"When your son was found, he was laying at the foot of a cross that, from what it looked like, he had just put up. Can you tell me what he was doing?"

Betty Carr sat up, still holding onto her husband for support as she looked deep into his eyes. When Randy gave a nod, Betty told the Lieutenant a brief story about how their son had met and fallen in love with a girl, and that this girl had died at that spot at the corner of Edgewood and Roosevelt while awaiting a school bus.

"Our son petitioned the City Counsel for permission to put up a cross where Catlin had died. It was her cross he had just put into place," Betty Carr explained.

"I've lived on the west side of town for the last fifty years and can't remember any kind of school bus stop at that corner," Lieutenant Berryman said.

"As a child, we would attend the theater there on Saturdays for twenty-five Coke-Cola bottle caps during the afternoon. Thinking back now, I do seem to remember hearing something about a school bus accident, but that was forty or fifty years ago. I've been a cop for the past thirty years and the west side has always been my beat, I can't remember any such accident since that one long ago," he told them.

"Well, I guess you've filled in as many pieces as you could, and I appreciate your time and information, if you can think of anything else, please call me. My cell phone number is on the back of the card," referring to the business card he had given each when they first met.

"We'll do that," Randy said and added, "Thank you for everything."

Pastor Snowden, who had stepped away for a few minutes returned and the three of them sat quietly in the little chapel until the nurse returned with Randy's insurance card asking both to sign a consent form.

"I'm gonna stay here. You'd better go home and see to the girls. I've got my cell phone on and will call you if there's any change."

"Okay," Randy agreed. "What do I tell them?

"I don't know," Betty said honestly. "They have a right to know. We're both needed here, and we're both needed there.

"Oh Randy," she cried softly, "how can this be happening? We've taken such care?" and she buried her face in his chest again.

Tears welled up in both of their eyes as they held on to one another. After a few minutes, Randy tore himself away saying, "I'd better go. I know the girls are worried sick too."

"Maybe you'd better pick up something from McDonald's on the way. It's late and I'm sure no one has given a thought about eating dinner," Betty reminded him as he walked towards the door.

Before Randy had the chance to leave the room, Pastor Snowden spoke to them both. "I know how hard this is on you. Randy told me of his sisters and how much he loved them. I'll be here should you need me," then turned to leave when Randy called him back.

"Pastor, our family has never been church goers, and if Randy doesn't make it through this, will you help?"

"I thought you knew," Pastor Snowden said.

"Knew what?" Betty asked.

"I'm the Pastor of the Westside Baptist Church. I'm one of the local pastors here at the hospital. We normally are called on in cases like this. Randy had my card in his shirt pocket and the hospital called me in when he first arrived. We had spoken to one another only a few hours ago, when he told me of his plans. Your son is and was not only a good boy, but I believe he was a special person as well, or he might not have ever met Catlin. A son you have every right to be proud of. I know I'm proud of him," Pastor Snowden offered. "Whatever I can do to help you get through this, just know I will be there for all of you. I think that is something Randy would want me to do for him."

Thanking the pastor, Randy left heading home to a house full of very scared children.

The nurse came in and announced, "We've moved your son to I.C.U. so we can better monitor his progress."

"Can I be with him?" Betty asked.

"Yes, ma'am, that's the reason we moved him. The doctor is making arrangements to bring in several teams of surgeons, should they be needed," she said. "He's in room 328."

Entering room 328, Betty noted several things. First was several "beeps" coming from the heart monitoring machine. There was a breathing machine next to it with a pump that went up and down filling Randy's lungs with oxygen. The room smelled of being just sanitized. The lights were turned down low, there was a single window and its curtains were thick and pulled closed.

Randy's bed was central to the room's back wall, which was covered with cream colored wall paper. There was a single black leather chair, a nightstand and what is called a mobile tray-table just to the right side of his bed, next to the chair that held a bucket of crushed ice, a pitcher of water, along with several plastic cups and two straws. The carpet was flush grey. It matched both the bed frame and the portable night stand which was stainless steel.

Looking at Randy, his face was totally relaxed. There wasn't a mark on him anywhere that Betty could see, but she knew the sheet and quilt covered the bandages on his chest. She watched as his chest rose and fell. It was hard to believe he was dying, and there wasn't anything she could do to help him.

Betty pulled the chair over to the side of the bed and sat down; took several deep breathes just to keep from crying, then stood and bent over her son and gently kissed Randy on his forehead, and again on his cheek. She noted how warm his skin was, then, as she sat back down, she put her hand over his, intertwining his fingers between her own. Betty hoped with all of her heart that Randy would say, "Mom, I'm too big for you to hold my hand like this," just once again. "Please God, let him come back to us."

"A twitch, Son. That's all I ask. Just let me know that you know it's me. Please, Randy," she pleaded. "If you can hear me, show me you want to live," the tears flowed freely.

Betty kissed his hands repeatedly as she cried and prayed and pleaded with God to spare her only son.

Slowly and quietly a nurse entered the room. She didn't want to interfere, but she had her job to do, and now it was to record all the numbers on the monitors and take his temperature and blood pressure. Then, she noticed that all the tissues were used and opened a drawer on the night stand and took out another of the small boxes, opening it and handing the box to Betty, then left the room. Neither woman said or had to say a word.

As the nurse left, Pastor Snowden came through the door. He too didn't want to bother her, and just placed his hand on her shoulder to let her know she wasn't alone.

Without the need for looking up or around, Betty's sixth sense seemed to tell her who was with her and she put her hand over his and asked,

"Pastor Snowden, why is this happening to us? Randy has never caused anyone any trouble. He is such a good boy, always there when someone needs a hand. Why him? Why now? He has worked so hard to get to where he's at. God can't need him that bad, can he?"

In answer, Hank Snowden said, "Your son, our Randy, seems to have a greater calling than that which awaited him here. Whatever plan the good Lord has in store for him, it's not to be here in our world. I feel sure that wherever God puts Randy, his visit here in our time and space on this world was to help him for his afterlife," Pastor Snowden told her.

"You know," Betty said, never taking her swollen eyes off of Randy, "my son had a girlfriend who died over forty years ago. A girl who appeared to have come back from the grave and Randy fell completely in love with her," then added, "we all fell in love with her. Catlin was like a missing part of our family tree. I can't explain it," Betty went on, "but let me ask you this, is it possible that she came back for Randy?"

"I really don't believe in *ghosts*, per say, but during my lifetime, I've learned that God does indeed work in some very mysterious and strange ways, using whatever means He needs and sees fit to carry out what He wants done," Pastor Snowden told her softly.

"Randy told me about his Catlin. I can't say he is with her right now,

203

but I want to believe he is well on his way to her on whatever plane God is directing him to go."

"Is that Heaven?" Betty asked innocently.

Pastor Snowden said, "What is Heaven if not a higher plane than this? According to the Bible, it says that God promises us that Heaven is to be here on Earth, not some other world. So perhaps," he said, "Heaven is nothing more than another, yet, a greater plane, something like a separate, but different dimension co-exiting with our own."

Giving much thought to what the Pastor said gave Betty some comfort as her tears and sobs subsided.

"What about Hell," Betty asked. "Is there truly a Hell where bad people go when they die?"

"My own personal feelings are like this, there wouldn't be much hope for mankind if there was only Heaven. There would be little thought of salvation if man didn't have the devil to think about, so I suppose," Pastor Snowden went on, "that God must indeed have a special Hell for those most deserving. That's not to say that all sinners will go to Hell, but surely there is such a place for those who reject God's love and Grace. After talking to Randy many times. I'm sure God will give him Grace with an abundance of his love," Pastor Snowden finished.

For the next twenty minutes, Betty and Hank Snowden prayed for

Randy, and again for Catlin. It was then that Randy Senior showed up with Tamara in tow saying, "Mary and the twins are downstairs. I told her I will come for her in twenty minutes.

Pastor Snowden suggested, "I think I can persuade the hospital to relax the rules and allow the twins to come up, if you'd like me to."

"Thank you," Betty told him. "That would be great."

Thinking, Betty asked, "Did you remember to call the Hydes. They'd be very hurt if we didn't let them know what was happening to Randy?"

"No," Randy told her honestly. "I'll go call them now."

Tamara was crying and seemed confused as she told her mother, "I don't understand."

Taking Tamara into her arms, Betty asked gently, "About what, dear?"

"I can't see anything wrong with him. He looks like he's just asleep. How can he be dying?" she asked.

"I know, I thought the same thing. According to the Doctor, the car hit him so hard, it collapsed one lung and caused his heart to stop.

"By the time they got the car off of him, and before they could start CPR, there hadn't been enough oxygen to his brain," Betty explained.

Then she pointed to one of the monitors and said, "That machine shows any activity in Randy's brain."

"But," Tamara started to say, "it's just a straight line," as it slowly sank in just what that line really meant.

Tamara was almost an honor student and had planned on going into nursing after college. She had watched all the most popular television shows like Scrubs, House, and most of the others. On each show, they showed what such a straight line really meant, she just didn't want something like that to be real, even though she knew that the shows portrayed real life experiences. She just never thought it would happen to her only brother.

Betty was saying something, but Tamara had been lost in her own thoughts. "I'm sorry, Mom, what were you saying?"

"I was saying that the doctors are keeping Randy alive so they can keep his organs alive for the transplants," Betty told her.

"You remember how Randy always talked about if something should ever happen he wanted to be a donor.

"Under the law, Randy's body must be kept alive if possible for a full twenty-four hours before anyone can take parts to be used to help save the life of another," Betty told her.

"So, " she went on, "sometime tomorrow, unless there is some change in his brain waves, about ten highly skilled surgical teams and eight or nine people who need organs will be arriving to transplant Randy's lung, kidneys, and liver and other things which will help them live. Then, they will begin taking Randy off life support, and if he can't breathe on his own, your father and I will give our consent and our Randy will be gone, but only to live his life through others, who would surely die without his help. We believe that this is what Randy would want us to do. Don't you agree?" Betty asked.

"Will we be able to meet the people whose livese he will be helping?" Tamara asked.

"Yes," Betty told her, "but only after their operations."

"So, in a way, Randy won't really be dead, just a small part of him will be gone, right?" Tamara said with finality.

Hugging her daughter for being so grown up and understanding about the loss of her brother, Betty could only take heart and was better able to accept her loss, too.

It was twenty minutes later when the Hydes arrived. Having worked at the Edgewood Memorial Hospital as a private duty nurse, Iris already knew the hospital and most of the staff.

Randy met them at the first door and led them upstairs and through the hospital to the I.C.U. wing where Betty and Tamara sat with Randy on the third floor.

Without asking, or waiting to be told, Iris automatically picked up the boys chart from the nurse's Station and brought it into Randy's room. She studied the chart for a few minutes, then turned pale white. Her heart sunk.

Randy Carr hadn't just been a passing boy in the short time she and Michael had known him. They had quickly grown to love him as a son they couldn't have, and now this was happening all over again. First, it was Catlin, and now it was Randy. *"Would he find the peace Catlin couldn't?"* she wondered.

It was then that Iris's training kicked in, and she calmly stated the facts. "Doctor English has begun asembling his staff of specialized surgeons and the hospital has eight recipients enroute from around the state. I think they plan to start about noon tomorrow," Iris told them.

"I want to stay with him as long as possible," Betty told her.

"Let me go talk to the head of the hospital, and see how long I can get," Iris said, and then left the room.

"Honey," Randy Senior told Tamara, "I think you'd better go relieve Mary with the twins."

Touching her brother's hand, Tamara got up from her chair, bent over Randy and kissed him on the forehead, knowing that this would be the last time she would ever see her brother alive.

Turning to leave, Tamara said to her father, "His hand is so warm, I thought it would be colder," then remembered that he was still on life-support. She kissed her mother and father and headed out the door.

Iris came back ten minutes later and said, "You can stay for about an hour, they have a lot of tests to run on him and on those who might be receiving his gifts," explaining, "everything must match, or his host could reject the organs."

It was then that Pastor Snowden came back in with Mary just behind him.

Mary had changed from the shorts she usually wore around the house to a dress. The blue print was multicolors of blue and white, with a medium cut front lined with a soft white lace on both the collar as well as on the midcut short sleeves.

She didn't know why she felt that wearing a dress was more appropriate than the shorts, but something in her told her to change. She felt better for it, but her mother didn't even notice. *"I guess she has more on her mind than whether I am wearing a dress or not,"* she thought to herself.

Her rust colored hair was highlighted with a matching ribbon, which again, she hadn't worn in ages, but being only twelve, she never gave thought to wearing make-up, or lip gloss, and her skin was too clear and young to need a covering agent for such things as blemishes and pimples. The dress and make-up did make her feel a few years older, and she felt this was the time she needed to feel that way. With her demeanor, you'd have thought she was the older between her and Tamara.

The twins who had been outside playing had been cleaned up and put in identical clothing with one exception, one blouse said, "Hi I'm Trish and the other said, Hi, I'm Tish."

Betty had little more than an hour left to relive every detail of Randy's life. From his first step to his first word, every detail was vivid in her mind's eye.

The time seemed to crawl by in increments. At first the time seemed to never change, but as the last hour of Randy's life ticked away, she was lost in the moment of every minute of his young life. Soon, all too soon, she would be saying goodbye, and that thought brought forth more tears; tears that Mary had taken notice of and closed her arms around her as though she could somehow protect her mother from the hurt and pain.

Sitting beside his wife, Randy too was trying to fill a lifetime of tomorrows in his son's last moments, Randy's first Birthday cake, he put his entire face into while trying to blow out a single, oversized candle. They must have laughed for half a day on and off.

Randy would relive his son's life every day, wondering if by some chance he might forget what might be a minor detail he would want to recall later.

Each member of young Randy Carr's family spent that long agonizing hour in remembrance of Randy, and how his life impacted not only each of their lives on an individual basis, but collectively as a family. Each knowing and vowing never to forget a young life cut short by a tragic accident.

It was almost eight o'clock, and the entire family was led to the small hospital chapel by Pastor Snowden, where they waited never knowing the exact moment of Randy's death; but knowing in their hearts that death had already claimed him long before they arrived at the hospital.

"What cannot be changed must be endured," Randy thought as he had had the responsibilities of taking care of his parent's funerals and later having to go through each person's personal properties, keeping precious keepsakes and dispensing of the rest of whatever possessions that remained. Now he was thinking of the hurt and pain he would have to endure as he thought of having to go through Randy's things. It would be a task he knew he had to do himself, and no matter what, he would do what had to be done, but not tonight.

Turning to Pastor Snowden, Randy asked, "Can you help with the

211

arrangements? This is all happening too fast and I can't think straight yet."

"I'll make some phone calls. There is a local funeral home that I've used in cases like this. Does your insurance plan give you cemetery plots? The director will need to know where you'll want him interned," Pastor Snowden asked.

"I don't remember," Randy answered honestly, then remembered he had bought four burial plots at the National Cemetery on Blanding Blvd, and told this to the caring Pastor.

A uniformed police officer came in the Chapel to clear up some paperwork and said, "We discovered your son's car in a parking lot next to the Edgewood Theater. It'll have to be moved, or we'll have to have it towed."

It seemed like a cold-blooded statement at the time, but it was the man's job, and it had to be taken care of, even in a situation like this, Randy thought to himself.

Randy's response was automatic and without malice. "I have a set of keys at the house. I'll move it later if that's alright?"

It was, and then the officer asked about some other minor details and handed Randy a small packet as he left.

"What's that?" Betty asked.

Handing the packet to his wife, Randy said, "I don't know."

Opening it, Betty found her son's wallet, watch, cell phone, and other items he must have been carrying at the time the EMT's had to rip off his clothes that had been placed in the envelope when he reached the hospital.

Another tear, another pause as Betty wrapped her arms around her husband who was already holding her as close as he could, but was now even closer to his wife.

Iris came over and said, "It's time for us to go."

"Go where?" Betty and Mary asked.

"Perhaps we'd all better go home, take a bath, and get some food to eat. They're gonna be twenty hours or more, and there is nothing here we can do to help," Iris explained.

Looking at each other, and then at their daughters, they felt very tired and drawn. It was then that both Randy and Betty realized they still had children to tend to, and that all had been up all night. Food had never been given a thought.

Betty hugged her new friend who reminded her so much of her own mother and said, "You're right. The twins are climbing the walls and must be starving."

"Will they call us when it's over?" Tamara asked.

"I'm going home for awhile and will come back about six tonight. I'll stay and contact you in the morning after the doctors are done," Iris promised, then shepherded them down the hall with their sleepy children.

"Is there anything we can do?" Randy asked. "Perhaps we could donate some blood," he suggested.

"Blood is always in need and forever in short supply, but you can do that another time," Iris told him. "Right now, you all need food and rest."

After picking up Michael from the lounge, they headed for the parking lot. Randy and Betty took their tired family home. On the drive, there was little talking and some very long faces.

Michael went with Randy after dropping the family off at home to pick up Randy Junior's pride and joy, then followed Randy back to the house, parked the Mustang in the garage, and closed the garage door.

After feeding the girls a simple breakfast, Betty and Iris put the girls down. It had been a long, long night, and the coming day promised to be longer yet. Getting everyone settled, Iris and Michael took their leave, and Randy and Betty headed for the shower in their room. Randy took a short cold shower and turned the room over to his wife who really didn't want a shower, and settled for a hot bath.

Sometimes, the best words are those left unspoken. No words could explain away the pain nor could any shower or bath.

Settling into the hot tub, Betty just laid there, letting the hot water run just enough to help keep the water as hot as she could stand.

Allowing his wife her privacy, Randy prepared for bed by turning down the quilt and comforter, then just sat in total silence for fifteen minutes. Getting up, he headed for the bathroom.

Seeing Betty half asleep, Randy took down a bottle of her favorite shampoo and knelt down saying, "Let me shampoo your hair," and then leaned over her head and gently kissed her.

Slipping down, dunking her head under the water, Betty slid back up and sat up allowing her husband a free reign to wash her hair. It was then that she realized just how tired she had become saying, "I don't think I had the energy to do that by myself."

Sitting up in the tub, she allowed Randy the room he always used as he got up and sat on the edge of the tub with his feet in the water, with his feet on either side of his wife where Betty leaned back against him and almost fell asleep as he gently washed the long brown hair he had always loved to touch and massaged her scalp and head.

Neither were in any hurry and needed the quiet comfortable assurance

215

of the other's presence. The tension that each felt took a long time to melt away, but as the old saying goes, "time heals all wounds" and Randy thought to himself, "time will never erase the memory of his only son, no matter how long time takes."

After half-an-hour, when he had washed her hair and back, and had finished rinsing her with the warmth of the hot water, he helped her out of the tub where she allowed him to pamper her as he took her long fluffy towel and caressed her body with his gentle drying off.

Taking his sleepy wife into the bedroom, he laid her down on the soft bed and neither had any thoughts of putting on bed clothes as he tucked her into her side of the bed.

Before getting in beside her, Randy picked up his robe, wrapping it around himself, and stepped out of the room turning off the light as he stepped into the hallway. He knew Betty was already sound asleep.

Randy first tip-toed into the room of his twins, quietly approaching each bed, retucking and kissing each before partly closing their door as he reentered the short hall.

Entering Mary's room, he noticed that her night light was still on. He then saw that Tamara was sound asleep. Randy looked again at Mary and saw that she was in fact still awake.

Going to her, he sat down on the side of her bed, and didn't say a word.

Mary, while still having her eyes closed, knew who had sat down and pulled herself up and into her father's arms. Nothing needed to be said between them. Like his wife, Randy knew every part of his daughter's heart and soul. He knew that she, more than any other member of the family, needed his kind and loving embrace.

After holding her in his arms for less than five minutes, Randy felt her slip into a deep sleep. Laying her down, he pulled the bed sheet up to her chin and slipped out of the room.

Back in the hallway, Randy went to the next room; the room of his namesake. He didn't know what to expect as he opened the door and turned on the lamp next to Randy's desk which sat next to the door.

Standing there, he slowly looked at the neat and all too quiet room. On the walls were pictures of Randy's favorite football players and his team of teams, the Jacksonville Jaguars. When the city finally got a football team of their own, the Dolphins were history in this part of the state, and very few residents ever got excited over the Bucs.

Randy remembered the first time he had taken his son to his first ever game, both father and son felt that because of this one move, Jacksonville had become a city of note.

While Jacksonville had a hockey team, a huge wrestling following, and its Jacksonville Suns, the city was always a minor league type city. All that changed with the Jags. Suddenly, the city was a major player in the sports arena and was hoping to land a basketball team during the next expansion in the near future.

Soon, there was arena football and things just continued to grow, and Randy Junior wanted to be a part of its future; now, he could only be a very small part of its past.

Randy Junior loved sports, he loved going to each game and kept all the paraphernalia he bought at each, tacking flags and pennants and fingers around his room. But like father like son, neither were any good at playing the game. Randy had caught one baseball while at the park when the Tidewater Tides was visiting the Suns, and both teams signed the ball for him. Randy proudly displayed the ball on the top of his desk.

Football and basketball and even wrestling had their pennants and paraphernalia, but only baseball had a real souvenir. Once caught, the catcher was allowed to keep it. "You can't do that in any other sport," Randy told his father.

Looking closer around his son's room, he found newly framed pictures of the only girl he ever brought home or ever mentioned in his life that meant something special to him.

Catlin was on his nightstand, his desk next to the famed baseball. He even had a picture of her blown up   by a friend hung over his bed. Losing her in so many ways really did kill him.

Not feeling any blame towards the girl because she gave Randy so much love in their short relationship, he could only remember how empty he felt when, as a boy his own son's age, he learned of 'his' Catlin's death only to relive her life and death through the eyes and heart of his own son.

He must have sat there with his head in his hands. He hadn't realized he had been crying until a warm hand was placed on his shoulder.

"I know," a voice softly said. "I know." The scent was all wrong.

Turning his face towards the voice, Randy saw Betty coming through the door. Glancing around the room, Betty came to him as he turned, sitting on his lap.

Nuzzling his face into her bosom, Randy told her, "Catlin was just here. She spoke to me."

"Oh my God," Betty said looking around the still empty and quiet room. "Are you sure?"

"She put her hand on my shoulder and said, "I know." He told her then when I looked up, you were coming through the door.

"I could smell her scent, the warmth of her hand."

"Do you think she'll come back?" Betty asked.

"For some reason I can't explain, I don't think so," Randy told her, "No, I don't think she'll come back."

"She's here for Randy, isn't she?" Betty asked more of a statement than a question.

"Possibly," was about all Randy could think to say.

Standing up and looking around the room, both parents of Randy Carr Junior had tears in their eyes as they quietly closed the door behind them heading back down the hall to their own bedroom.

℧

The telephone rang and it seemed the entire household woke up. By the third ring, all the children had entered their parent's bedroom.

"Hello," Randy Senior answered. "Yes, I understand. Thank you for letting us know, Iris. How soon will they move him?"

"I'll call Pastor Snowden and let him know, and Iris," Randy said as he looked over at his four daughters and wife, "Thank you again for all your help."

There are many things about life a parent will accept as true, but the loss of a child is still challenged, even until the child is laid to rest.

Hanging up the phone, the four children climbed into their parent's bed not saying a word, not needing to. The hugs and tears came freely and flowed freely by each, parent and child alike, until all had fallen into a deep sleep, holding on to each other, each fearing to open their eyes to the reality of the harsh cruel world.

℘

The following morning, life began anew in the Carr household. Slowly each child got hungry, and Betty started to cook. School for the remainder of the year was forgiven and forgotten since there were only nine days left in the year.

Randy had taken two weeks off from work so that he could be there for each of his family's need, whatever that need might entail; not to forget the feelings of his own loss that needed to be soothed and comforted.

The ice cold fresh orange juice Tamara made, while as good as always, seemed to lack something. The conversation was light because nobody wanted to mention Randy's name. Even the twins, as lively as they always were, were still quiet and subdued in their talk and actions. But life did go on, even if in a slower pace.

After their first breakfast together, Mary helped with the dishes, something she rarely did, while Tamara took the twins upstairs for a quick bath in which she allowed them the use of some of her special bath beads, and shampooed each young girl's hair. After drying them off, she spent the next hour brushing each one's hair to a soft sheen.

Not knowing what this first day at home without their brother would be like, or who might come by, Tamara put matching dresses on them, telling them the importance of staying clean and playing as quietly as possible as not to disturb their parents as they went through the matters of an unusual day, explaining that no one would be playing outside anyway, at least not for today saying, "Just try to stay clean, okay?"

It was just after nine A.M. when the door bell rang; Mary got there first. She too was wearing a dress. It was a full length navy blue that ended just above her ankles. It had no print to it, but was trimmed in old fashioned lace. Her hair was almost black, which cast her in a somber mood, but was held by a barrette her brother had bought for her last year at Christmas.

"I'm sorry," was all Iris and Michael could say as they came into the living room. Michael carried two dozen bright yellow roses of Texas. We thought he'd like these," he handed the vase to Mary.

Iris was carrying a rather large covered dish and lead Betty towards the kitchen saying, "You're gonna need to eat later," placing the casserole in the oven and turning it on a low temperature.

The door bell rang again and Randy got there first. It was a neighborhood florist who told Randy that he had several deliveries for them.

It seemed that within minutes the house was alive with people and flowers. Friends, neighbors, and over a dozen of Randy's closest classmates and the entire office staff of the law office was there. Almost everyone brought food and/or flowers and cards.

No one in the Carr family was left alone. The talk covered every aspect of Randy's short life span and how he brought enrichment to each of their lives and days.

The day wore on and Pastor Snowden joined them at midday. Iris, along with Betty and Tamara spent much of their time preparing sandwiches for everyone.

Randy wondered where everyone would sit, but it seemed to him that every person found their nitch and everyone had plenty of room and food, even the twins were well taken care of, entertained, fed and cleaned.

"I've made arrangements with Grey Funeral Home for a viewing before the funeral, which I think should be held day after tomorrow," Mr. Smith and Pastor Snowden told Randy and Betty.

They agreed.

The memory of Randy Carr Junior continued to be talked about throughout the rest of the day.

Iris, Betty, Mrs. Smith, Tamara, Mary, Wendy and another half dozen women took turns cleaning up and putting things away. By seven P.M., the household was basically tired and worn out. As the last of the more than two dozen visitors left, the twins had had their baths and were in deep sleep.

Mary and Tamara were tired and ready for an early bed.

"You'll want to drop by the church about eight in the morning to help set up the wake in the chapel," Pastor Snowden suggested as he, too, made his way out the front door.

"Thank you for all your help," Randy told him closing the door behind him.

In a way, it didn't seem that the first day of young Randy's death lasted long enough to his family, but all were thankful when they laid their heads down on their pillows for the night that it was behind them for the moment.

At the church the next morning, things felt surreal. The funeral home arrived at five minutes before eight, and by eight-thirty, Randy Senior had emptied the car of all the flowers.

Since the death of Betty's mother had occurred just a year before, he had remembered helping arrange the flowers; keeping those she loved the most closest to the casket. He simply followed suit in arranging the flowers for his son.

"It's funny," Betty told Mary, "I hadn't really realized what kind of flowers Randy liked, let alone which might be his favorites."

"It's easy," Mary told her. "You always loved the 'yellow rose of Texas' being the brightest of the yellow roses, he knew that and because you loved it, he loved it even more."

"Almost any solid bright color went with anything you wore, as he always bought you what made you smile. Knowing that they made you smile made his heart glad," Mary told her mother.

The funeral home people had gone to the house the afternoon before while everyone else was busy and Betty and Tamara picked out a suit for Randy to wear. Both were glad they wouldn't have to dress him as they might have had to just a few years before.

The casket remained closed, though it had been opened several times upon request by each of the Carr family.

Eyes closed, Randy laid in total peace. "It doesn't look like the hospital took anything," Tamara remarked to her younger sister, Mary.

"I'm just glad I didn't have to see all the cuts on him, Mary said.

By nine A.M., Iris and Michael had arrived, and Randy's funeral began at ten. Five minutes before, Wendy and Steve had arrived wearing a new engagement ring Steve had given her the night before.

It was decided on that Steve and each of the other interns from the law office would act as pallbearers.

"I didn't know Randy had so many friends," Randy Senior noted to Pastor Snowden. "I guess I lost touch with his life, thinking I was taking care of the family."

Thinking about his words after just speaking them he reflected, "That's a very poor excuse for not knowing who Randy liked or was with. I'll remember to pay more attention to each of the girls from here on," he promised himself.

Two days later, it took an hour and a half to reflect on Randy's life during the short church service. When it was over, the procession began when Pastor Snowden allowed each of his family one last good-bye and then he closed the lid to the casket.

All of Randy's friends from work and school that had been chosen to be his pallbearers lifted his casket, carrying it to the shiny new Cadillac hearse where with the help from the driver and his assistant, secured it in the rear of the car, placing the flowers that remained at the church over the casket.

More than a hundred cars, carrying over three hundred people moved along Roosevelt southwest towards Blanding Boulevard There was no hurry and the drive took more than an hour. The second car carried most of the floral arrangements. The cemetery had already set up the tent. Being a Thursday, the tent was green. Each day's events used a different color. Sunday was yellow, Monday was blue, Tuesday was red, Friday orange, and Saturday was white.

Pulling into the cemetery, the caravan was met by a brown motorized golf cart that led the procession to the plot Randy and Betty had purchased four years before.

The hearse pulled up to the site and the attendants got out and opened the rear door where the pallbearers gathered. They carried Randy's casket to the waiting arms of the rack that would hold him until after the ceremony and where, with the push of a single button, his remains would be lowered back into the ground that once gave him life.

The attending friends and family gathered around the small hole which was covered by a carpet and a tent to say good-bye as Pastor Snowden lead them in the Lord's Prayer.

"Ashes to ashes, dust to dust, we give back the body of Randy Carr Junior, but only his body do we return to our Mother Earth. Randy's heart and soul that made him the man and person he grew to be, will remain in our hearts and minds forever." Then he pushed the button and Randy's body was lowered into the ground.

At the head of the grave was a solid granite stone of slate gray that was inscribed with Randy's name, date of birth and death with the simple words of his parents,

HERE LIES OUR ONLY SON
HE BROUGHT HAPPINESS
AND
LAUGHTER INTO OUR LIVES
REST IN PEACE

Randy, Betty, the girls and Iris and Michael were the last to leave and once Pastor Snowden saw it was time, he led them back to the limo and the long ride home.

"Home is such an empty sounding word," Betty remarked as the limo finally pulled into their driveway. The tears were still there just long cried out.

"It's been a long day," Randy said quietly as he thanked the driver and signed the receipt.

Iris and Michael stayed on the front lawn and then for only a few minutes before getting into their own car for the ride home with a promise to call them the next day.

Entering the house, Betty and Tamara put the twins down for a long needed nap. The mood remained subdued the rest of the day and into the night.

℘

The grounds crew at the cemetery filled in the grave and neatly arranged the flowers as they had so many times before and left for the day.

The following morning, when the crew showed up for work, they met as always at the manager's office to go over the day's schedule. There was a barn of sorts behind the office where they refueled the golf cart, then headed off to begin more than two dozen new grave sites that were ready for sodding. Young Randy's would be the last added to the list, and would be leveled the following day.

The barn that held their tools and equipment was on the backside of the chapel. The clipboard that held their job assignments was always on a nail just inside of the barn. The cemetery manager wouldn't be in for another two hours.

It took about forty-five minutes to check out the equipment and see to the first twelve squares of sod being loaded in the wagon being towed by the golf cart.

The first grave they were to remove the tent and rake the ground smooth was that of Randy Carr. It would take two more days before sod could be added and it was also the grave closest to the chapel.

The ground crew consisted of eight people, six men and two women. David Pyle was the most senior of the workers. His job was to see each plot of land cleared and set so that only they and the immediate family would know the ground wasn't broken.

It's hard to start a fresh day and run into a problem within the first hour, and David Pyle wasn't ready for the kind of problem he would face this morning.

Less than ten thousand feet from the chapel the morning before, David Pyle and Sandra Goldberge had set up the green tent for the boy who was buried the day before.

As David Pyle and Sandra Goldberge had set up the green tent, it was also up to them to take it down, and store it back in the barn, but since Sandra was off today, David chose another helper, a young Mexican-born eighteen year old named Hector Morales to help take the tent down and straighten out the site before any visitors dropped by. The wind the night before was blowing pretty hard and David was sure that a lot of things had been blown off the grave. They always did.

When they left the barn, David was sure he could see the tent because it really wasn't all that far from the chapel, yet, when they rounded the corner, the tent was nowhere in sight."I guess the wind was stronger than I thought," he told the young boy next to him.

David had worked in cemeteries much of his life, totaling over sixteen years. He had also worked for many other cemeteries around the country. He liked this one because it was a National Cemetery and showed honor towards the Veterans they buried there. It was a good place to be interned, and it was also part of his job to make sure that the graves were well taken care of. He taught his crew that every site must be maintained in the same respectful manner, Veteran or not.

When they reached the site, he knew immediately that something was very wrong. At first, he thought that someone had already taken down the tent or that it might have been blown down, but no one was told to do so. Then he noticed that there were no flowers and that it looked at first like the gravesite had been covered with sod. He was starting to get very upset with his crew, that is until he looked closer at the site itself.

It was then that he noticed that the ground itself had not yet been broken, meaning it had never been dug into. Yet, the day before he and his helper had themselves buried the young Carr boy into the ground at their feet.

He was gone, the grave was gone, the boy and his body were gone and the ground was still virgin.

Since the young Mexican had not worked the site, David sent him on to do something else saying, "I've got to go to the office. You go help Sam, he is on the other side driving the red cart, and I'll pick you up later after I check on a few things."

Then the boy disappeared and David headed for the office.

It was David's job to check each grave site and since he knew where the hole was he had dug the day before, he knew where he was going, or so he thought.

David rechecked the chart in the main office where he had put the blue pin in the grave site to indicate the grave was being used; only the chart board didn't show any such pin or the hole where the pin should have been.

"Mr. Farr," David spoke into the phone. He went on and before Mr. Farr could even get a word out, David asked, "How soon before you can get here?"

"Is there a problem?" Frank Farr asked, sensing something in the voice and realizing that David had never called him at home before today.

"I'm not sure," David told him. "But something is amiss. Do you remember the burial of the young boy yesterday?"

"The one behind the chapel that belongs to the Carr family?" Mr. Farr asked.

"Yes, sir, that's the one," David answered.

"Okay, so what's wrong?" Farr asked.

"The problem is," David Pyle said "is…"

"Alright, David," Farr said, "what's the punch line?"

"Sir, I'm not kidding, the grave is not there. Neither is the gravestone I put there the night before," David told him again.

"David, if you're pulling my leg, you're gonna be in big trouble. I'll be there in half an hour," Farr told him.

After hanging up, David returned to his other duties, getting the digging machine out and fueling it and sharpening the edges and then moved the machine to the new site of the next hole to be dug, it would be needed the next morning, which was on the opposite side of the cemetery, so that Castillo and Mac could begin digging at first light, as the funeral for Dirk Rattle was for two P.M.

After loading the cat onto the trailer, he, Mac, and Rene Castillo drove out to the new site.

Climbing the winding path, David saw the missing tent. Before dropping Mac and Rene off, he had them go with him to find out how the tent got moved and to where.

Upon their approach, David noticed that the new grave, which he was sure none of his crew had dug, was covered with all the flowers he was sure he and Mac had placed on the site of the Carr boy's grave the day before.

Looking further, David also noticed a new white cross nearly touching

233

another cross on an older grave, yet both crosses were identical and new.

"Do you know anything about this new grave?" David asked his helpers.

"No, sir," both answered.

"When David looked at the name on the crosses and the name on the new grave, he almost fainted. "This has got to be some kind of joke," he said aloud.

David decided to leave everything just as he found it until Frank Farr got there. He knew whatever was happening was way beyond his pay scale, and sent his workers on to the Settle job site. There was no reason to involve them in this mystery.

Getting them situated, David returned to the small office to wait for his boss, as he went over again every aspect of what he was sure Frank would want to know.

With technology having advanced as far as it had, David Pyle took out his cell phone and took pictures of all he had seen and done, just as he had been doing the last two years.

Every day, David and Frank both documented their work with pictures and computer deposited composites of cemetery life.

Both had heard stories of ghosts, spirits, and strange things that have happened around graveyards, and keep their own records just in case. Today, David was glad he had done so.

There had been vandals who were out to destroy gravestones, digging up newly buried bodies looking for gold teeth or family jewelry, so pictures were the norm, and then stored on the computer for future use, should the case arise. David had never heard of a body ever being moved and a new head stone being placed on a grave.

When Frank Farr got to his office, he met with David and poured himself a cup of fresh decaf David had made just before he pulled in. Then he put his private password in his office computer, and the two of them went over every aspect of the Carr and Hyde funerals and burials.

"Mr. Carr," Frank said over the phone, after David showed him all that had taken place, "I need you and your wife to come in as soon as you can. There's been some vandalism, and before I call in the police, I need your advice."

Shock, despair and disbelief were written on Randy's face as he heard the news. Betty, who insisted that he take some time off to be with the family, almost turned pure white as she looked up at him from the living room sofa where they had been relaxing.

Tamara and Mary had been out of the house less than an hour when the phone rang. From the look on her husband's face, dread overcame her. Looking up at him, she barely got a single word out of her mouth loud enough for him to hear, "WHAT!"

Hanging up the receiver, Randy stood there not believing what he had just heard. Quietly, he sat down beside Betty who was now shaking on the sofa and for a few moments, just sat there not saying anything.

Scared half out of her wits, more afraid than she had ever been in her life at that moment repeated her earlier question, "WHAT, WHO," were her next words.

Composing himself and getting a little color back in his cheeks, Randy said "That was Frank Farr from the cemetery. There's been some vandalism at Randy's grave. He wants us both to come out right away," Randy told her still not believing the words coming out of his mouth.

"What kind of vandalism?" Betty asked as color came back to her face. The new color coming to her face was red.

"I don't know, but before he calls the police, he wants our advice as to how to proceed. I told him it would take us about an hour because we needed to find someone to watch the girls," Randy told her.

Picking up her cell phone, Betty called her best friend and neighbor, Nancy Higginbottom who lived next door. "Nancy," she said, "I need you to watch the twins for me. Tamara and Mary are out for the day. Randy and I have some legal business to take care of. I can drop them off in about twenty minutes, if that's alright? Thanks, I appreciate it," Betty said without explaining why they couldn't take the girls with them.

It took ten minutes to get dressed and get the girls ready to go, then they were out the door heading across the lawn towards Nancy's house.

Nancy was a petite woman of thirty with short cut strawberry blonde hair who barely stood five feet tall. She and her husband had three sons, the oldest was five years younger than Mary and lucky for her had other things on his mind besides girls.

She opened the door and Betty turned the girls over and then told her friend, "We'll be gone for a couple of hours. I'll call if we're to be any longer," then said, "thanks again, I owe you one."

Randy had already pulled the car out of the driveway and was waiting for her at the curb.

No words were spoken on the forty-five minute drive, each not knowing what they might find when they reached the cemetery. What Frank Farr hadn't told them was that he had also called Michael and Iris Hyde to come out at the same time, both arriving about the same time as the other.

Pulling in at the main office at the cemetery, Randy and Betty were very surprised to see Iris and Michael just starting to get out of their Toyota.

Seeing the Carrs drive up halted the Hydes from going in the office. "What are y'all doing here?" Iris asked.

"There seems to have been some trouble here last night, and Mr. Farr said Randy's grave was involved," Betty explained. "Why are you here?"

"Same reason, I guess," Michael answered. "Might as well see what damage has been done." Then the four people went in.

Entering, they found a spacious outer office with a desk that was cleared of any sign that anyone ever sat at it. They had not gone inside more than three steps when the manager, Frank Farr emerged from an inner office.

"Thank you for coming," Frank Farr said as he shook hands with each. "I'm sorry to have had to call you folks out here, but I'm in a dilemma and need your advice as to what to do," he said honestly.

"I don't think we quite understand," Randy said, "You said over the phone that there was some kind of vandalism?"

"It's not the type you normally would hear about, especially here at the National Cemetery where we have three guards roaming the grounds nightly," Frank told them.

"I'm afraid we still don't understand," Iris told him.

"Perhaps you'd better show us what you're talking about."

"Maybe that would be best," Frank agreed, then took them over to the bulletin board showing hundreds of pins over an overlaid map of the cemetery, showing each burial plot in the cemetery, and he pointed out where Catlin's plot was next to her parents', except, that there was now only two plots pinned instead of the three that the Hydes owned. Not only were there only two pins in the plots, but the red pins showed that there were two people already interned there, where it should have shown a single red pin and two white pins, one on either side of the red pin where Catlin lay.

Circling in a circular motion, Frank indicated what should have been their three sites, the sites were clearly shown to be in the far left rear corner of the cemetery because it was one of the first areas opened over forty years ago. Every ten years, a new section had been opened as needed, and each was color coded to match the year they became available to be used.

This much everyone understood, except that one pin on their plot was not only gone, but showed that the third plot had not been holed. "But this map has never been replaced, and," Frank told them, "yesterday, I'd have sworn there were two white pins on either side of the single red that is there now."

"How can it show another person being interned there now?" Michael asked.

"Because, there is in fact a second person buried there," Frank told them. "The problem is, we didn't bury anyone there yet, but there is a new person buried there today."

"What has that got to do with us," Betty asked.

Pointing to a series of burial plots on the opposite side of the cemetery, Frank showed them the four plots Randy and she had purchased several years before, and where Randy and she had seen with their own eyes just several days ago Frank had put a blue pin in place of one of the four white pins showing where Randy Junior was to be buried, explaining that, "After the funeral, my yard manager and/or I would replace the blue pin with that of a red one."

"So why are there only three pins there now?" Michael asked, "And why doesn't it show a fourth pin?" Then, rubbing his finger on the surface of the map, Michael said, "It's smooth, like there was never a pin ever put in it."

Well," Frank said, "that's part of the problem. There should be a red one there. I know David put it there, I was with him when he did it."

Looking at the whole of the board, there were no red pins anywhere near the plot that Randy had chosen, as it was a newly opened section, and his purchase was one of the first sold. "But there still should be four white pins that I watched you put in the map," Randy said.

"True, and that's another part of the mystery," Frank told them.

"Mystery?" queried Iris. "What mystery?'

"Maybe we'd best go out there so you can see for yourselves," Frank told them, then herded them out a side door where Frank had a large electric golf cart waiting, the same type vehicle Randy and Betty had ridden in when they first looked at the sites they chose several years before.

"I never thought I'd be visiting Randy's grave so soon," Betty told Iris as they sat in the back of the cart.

Frank Farr didn't say much on the way to Randy's gravesite of the day before. When they arrived about three minutes later, all were shocked to see not only unbroken ground with no headstone, but when Farr stopped at the four plots they had picked out, they were sure that this was the exact spot where they had seen the hole dug and Randy's body lowered into the day before. Iris thought that had Betty been standing, she might have fainted.

"Where is Randy?" she cried.

"That's what we're trying to figure out," Farr said, "but, as strange as this might seem, there is more."

Getting back into the cart, Frank Farr drove to where Catlin was buried and said, "This is what we found this morning."

Before them was a new grave, one that was covered with all the flowers they knew were the exact ones that they bought for Randy's grave.

Before them were two graves, one old, one new, both had a cross, each matching the other, both were no more than four inches apart. One had a yellow rose in its center vase, the newer one had a white rose in its center vase.

Between the two crosses, at the T was a single strand of pure gold, liken to a gold braid and hanging from the braid were two rings.

Looking at the first ring, all saw it was as new as it had been the day Catlin got it at Robert S. Lee High School only the week before her death. It had been buried with her forty years ago.

The other ring had Randy's name on it and it too looked as new as the day he had received it from the same school. Just before the casket was lowered, Betty had opened the casket and placed it on his right hand's third finger, the one he always wore it on.

His ring was on her side, her ring was on his side of the graves.

The inscription on Catlin's cross read, "Here lies Catlin Hyde, beloved daughter of Michael and Iris Hyde and beloved wife of Randy Carr Junior."

The second cross read, "Here lies Randy Carr Junior, son of Randy and Betty Carr, and beloved husband of Catlin Hyde."

The End

7:55 A.M.

HEAVEN CRIES

Weeping for the child
Whose heart is pure
As into this cruel world
He has a lifetime to endure

For the love of our Mother
And of our Father
And the things we do
To ourselves and to one another

As the skies grow dark
Saddened by dull clouds
Pillowed against each other
In silent shades of grey

For the things we have now
And for the things we want
Of the choices we make
Our future
They may haunt

So follow your heart
Don't wear a disguise
Be who you were meant to be
HEAVEN CRIES!

Douglas Vest

Lee Charles Daniels

7:55 A.M.

TIED TOGETHER AS ONE

A whisper of wind
Blows gently by, softly
Playing her name.

He sees the beauty
That existed then
Now only a silhouette
Through a lighted gown.

She was once loved
Then taken away
Leaving behind her soul
To a saddened heart.

Gone as time fell
To the rustle of leaves
Strengthened by the stones

Alone as two, yet tied
Together as one
Through their love
Shared decades ago.

Douglas Vest

AUTHOR'S BIO

Author Daniels with his wife and soul mate Mary Adele

Lee Daniels is a disabled Vietnam Nam Veteran. He has suffered the multiple sclerosis since 1992, but continues his love of the unknown.

An avid, reader, he enjoys all space adventures and seeks to better understand the mysteries of his home planet Earth.

He has written several documentaries, two dozen novels, and another twenty short stories.

He lives a quiet lifestyle in a guarded community near Beaumont, Texas.

You may comment on this book through leedbooks@hotmail.com.

Other books by Lee Charles Daniels:

Manta Ray

Man's quest to find his place in space and the struggle to secure it.

www.ingramcontent.com/pod-product-compliance
Lightning Source LLC
Chambersburg PA
CBHW070551130626
46556CB00001B/107